Jesse Bowman
A Union Boy's War Story

Tom McGowen

 Enslow Publishers, Inc.
40 Industrial Road
Box 398
Berkeley Heights, NJ 07922
USA

http://www.enslow.com

Copyright © 2008 by Tom McGowen

Library of Congress Cataloging-in-Publication Data:

McGowen, Tom.
    Jesse Bowman : a Union boy's war story / Tom McGowen.
      p. cm. — (Historical fiction adventures (HFA))
    Summary: At the age of seventeen, Jesse Bowman of Chicago joins the Union Army to fight in the Civil War, having only a romantic notion of what war is all about, but once he enlists he learns about both the tedium of daily life as a soldier and the hardships and cruelty of battle.
    ISBN-13: 978-0-7660-2929-3
    ISBN-10: 0-7660-2929-8
    1. United States—History—Civil War, 1861–1865—Juvenile fiction. [1. United States—History—Civil War, 1861–1865—Fiction.] I. Title.
    PZ7.M16947Je 2007
    [Fic]—dc22   2007005230

Printed in the United States of America

10 9 8 7 6 5 4 3 2 1

Illustration Credits: Enslow Publishers, Inc., p. 150; The Library of Congress, pp. 154, 156; National Archives and Records Administration, p. 152; National Park Service, p. 1 (background); Original painting by © Corey Wolfe, p. 1.

Illustration of Guns Used in Book Design: Schuyler, Hartley & Graham, *Illustrated Catalog of Civil War Military Goods,* published by Dover Publications, Inc., in 1985.

Cover Illustration: Original painting by © Corey Wolfe.

Contents

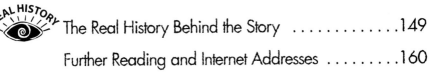

To Steve Snelten

chapter one

The Mighty Chicago Zouaves

O n the night of April 21, in the year 1861, a huge crowd was gathered around a large building in the city of Chicago, Illinois. In the crowd were two teenage boys. One of them was a tall boy with dark hair and eyes, named Jesse Bowman. He was sixteen years old. The other was smaller, with blond hair and blue eyes, a complete opposite to his companion. His name was Harlow Basset, and he was a few months younger than Jesse.

The building was an armory, a place where military units drilled, and Jesse, Harlow, and the rest of the crowd were there to watch a military unit march off to war. The unit was known as the Chicago Zouaves.

The Chicago Zouaves were one of the city's prides. They were a militia unit based on the very special, colorfully uniformed units of the French army. A Chicago newspaper had once described a Zouave as "a fellow who can climb a greased pole feet first, carrying a barrel of pork in his teeth—," and who, with a pistol in each hand, could "—knock the spots off a ten of diamonds at eighty paces, turning somersaults all the time."

At precisely ten o'clock, the two huge doors of the building were pulled open from the inside. There was a sudden roll of drumbeats and a clashing of cymbals, and bugles began to scream a brisk march tune. The Chicago Zouaves emerged. They formed three long lines, side by side, marching in perfect step. They wore short blue jackets with two rows of gold buttons, wide baggy red trousers, calf-high, white cloth leggings, and red round flat-topped caps with shiny black visors. The crowd clapped, cheered, and waved.

The Zouaves marched straight out into the middle of the street. There was a shouted command of "Column Right—MARCH!" The column turned with the smoothness of a slithering snake, each row of three men that formed a section of the three lines swung to the right, one after another. They now marched toward the lakefront to the Illinois Central Railroad depot.

Jesse had heard that the Chicago Zouaves and several other Chicago militia units were being ordered to the town of Cairo, down at the very tip of southern Illinois.

Although just a tiny town where two rivers joined, Cairo had suddenly become important because of its location.

For ten days, the United States had been divided into two sides, eight Southern states calling themselves the Confederacy, and nineteen Northern states and four border states calling themselves the Union. Three other Southern states seemed likely to secede. These two divisions of America were officially at war with each other, and Cairo was right on the border between them. In Northern hands, it could be a base for an invasion of the South. In Southern hands, it could become a base for invading the North.

Illinois had a great many people who had strong ties to the South, and it was possible some of them might well try to take over Cairo for the Confederacy. The governor of Illinois had decided it would have to be protected.

Most of the crowd was following behind the Zouaves. Jesse and Harlow also followed the march to the depot, then stood watching as the Zouaves said good-bye to family and friends. Jesse found himself envying these soldiers going off on an exciting adventure so unlike his boring daily life.

chapter two

Hearing the Call to Duty

Starting the next day, Jesse began scanning the paper each morning to see what was happening in the war. He was surprised that no battles seemed to be taking place. He questioned his father about this over breakfast one morning.

"You can't fight battles without armies, Jess," his father told him, smiling slightly. "Both we and the Southerners are trying to build up armies, and that means getting thousands and thousands of men together, training them to be soldiers, and giving them guns and cannons and horses." He shook his head. "It will take a long time before either side is ready to fight, and many people hope this terrible situation can be remedied so there won't be any fighting."

At school, most of the talk was about the war. The last war the United States had been involved in, the Mexican War, had ended thirteen years ago when even the oldest boys now at the school had been very young children. No students remembered anything about it. They wondered what it would be like to be at war.

There was a lot of talk among the boys about enlisting. "I'm going to enlist as soon as I can," boasted Henry Case, one of Jesse's friends. "I'm willing to fight to preserve the Union!"

"Fight to preserve the Union" was a phrase Jesse was hearing a lot lately. What it meant, he knew, was "Fight to put the Union back together." Jesse had been fifteen years old back in December 1860 when South Carolina had become the first Southern state to pull out of the Union. *Well, then, let it leave*, Jesse had thought at the time. What does it matter? Now, he saw that it had mattered. What had once been a proud, great nation was split into two bitterly opposed enemies. It now seemed to Jesse that enlisting to fight to try to put the Union back together might be a very worthwhile thing to do.

"I want to preserve the Union, too," declared Jim Robertson, another of Jesse's schoolmates, "but I sure don't want to preserve it the way it was. We've got to fix things so that there can't be any slavery anywhere in the Union any more."

"Are you an abolitionist, Jim?" asked Harlow Basset.

Jesse knew that the people called abolitionists wanted to see the North conquer the South because they thought slavery could then be abolished in the South. They believed slavery was a terrible, evil thing. Like many Northerners, Jesse did not much care whether slavery was abolished or not. He did not really know much about it. He had heard that Southerners believed it was a way of taking care of people who could not take care of themselves, and if that was true, maybe it was a good thing. But, being unsure about it, he did not think he could bring himself to enlist just to fight against slavery.

From the newspaper of June 17, Jesse learned that the Chicago Zouaves had returned to Chicago and would become the first two companies of a regiment, a military unit of about a thousand men, that was to be put into service that day. It would officially be known as the 19th Illinois Volunteer Infantry Regiment, and unofficially as the Chicago Zouaves. The last sentence in the newspaper article stated: "The regiment is looking for volunteers to enlist to bring it to full strength." Jesse read this sentence several times.

He continued to look through the newspaper every morning, to see if the 19th Illinois had been in a battle yet. However, there simply did not seem to be any battles being fought. Is this the way it is in every war, he wondered. Are there just months and months of nothing happening?

Then, on a morning in July, there were screaming headlines. There had been a battle at a place in Virginia called Manassas, only some twenty-five miles from Washington, D.C. The result of the battle had been a crushing defeat for the Union forces. Most of the Union Army at the battle had run away. If the Confederate troops had followed after them, they probably could have captured Washington, but apparently they had been confused and uncertain about what to do.

President Abraham Lincoln appointed a new general to command the army, and he began to vigorously train and reorganize it, but nothing more happened during the rest of the year.

The first month of 1862 was also peaceful. Then, in mid-February, the newspaper brought new news to Jesse. A Union army aided by gunboats captured a Confederate fort and fifteen thousand Confederate soldiers in Tennessee—a resounding Union victory. There was excitement in Jesse's school that day, for this was the first Union victory of the war. Several days later, city newspapers carried stories that thousands of Confederate prisoners were being sent to Chicago to be imprisoned in the large Union Army encampment there called Camp Douglas. Jesse, Harlow, and most of their schoolmates were quickly aware of this.

"Those Confederate prisoners will be coming in a couple of days," Harlow remarked to Jesse in their class that afternoon. "Why don't we go look them over, Jesse?"

"All right," Jesse said. "That should be something to see! Thousands of prisoners! I've sure never seen anything like that before."

After school on the day the first of the prisoners were to arrive, Jesse and Harlow took a horse-drawn street car to what was called the downtown part of the city and walked to the railroad depot. Thousands of other Chicagoans were gathered there.

As the prisoners came off the train, guarded by blue-clad Union soldiers, Jesse was shocked by their appearance. They did not look the least bit like soldiers. They were not dressed in uniforms; they were dressed in rags. The rags were not even all the remains of clothing. Some men were wrapped in tattered horse blankets, bed quilts, and pieces of rugs. Their shoes were coming apart. They were gaunt and looked starved. They trudged toward Camp Douglas, shivering and obviously suffering in the biting cold of a Chicago February. Jesse felt sorry for the prisoners.

In March and April there were battles that were clear victories for the North. Jesse was becoming worried. All these Union victories, plus the look of those ragged Confederate soldiers he had seen, seemed to indicate that the South was losing the war. Jesse was growing afraid that the war might be over before he could get into it. He was seventeen years old now, and if the war should end soon, he would never have the chance to take part in a great war and gain glory and honor for himself on the battlefield.

He finally decided he would enlist as soon as possible. It was easy to enlist, he knew—you just had to be tall enough, healthy enough, and a male. Age did not matter; he had heard of a fourteen-year-old who had enlisted. You did not need anyone's permission. He did not intend to tell his parents of his decision because he knew they would forbid him. He would simply go and do it, and once he was in, there was nothing they could do. Lots of boys ran away from home to enlist. The army did not care. It would not send them back.

He finally admitted to himself that he probably wanted to enlist mainly for the excitement and adventure of it. There was no excitement in his life. All he did was go to school and maybe read a book in the evening. He remembered how exciting it had been to see the Zouaves and other soldiers at the railroad depot, getting ready to go and protect Cairo. Something like that would be worth looking forward to! All he had to look forward to was boredom—finishing high school and then studying to be a lawyer, like his father. His parents had always wanted him to become a lawyer, but he could not bear the thought of spending the rest of his life drawing up wills for old people or writing deeds for people who were buying property.

Jesse's father seemed content with his work, but Jesse was sure he would not be.

He knew exactly what regiment he would enlist in—the 19th Illinois, the Chicago Zouaves!

He told Harlow of his decision. "I know where their recruiting station is," Harlow said, stroking his chin as if he were thinking about something. "It's on Dearborn Street, across from the post office."

"I'm going there on Saturday, then," Jesse said.

Harlow looked at him for a moment. Then finally he said, "I'll go with you, Jess. I want to enlist too."

Jesse felt his face break into an enormous grin. He clasped his friend's shoulder. "That's *Bully*, Harlow!"

On Saturday morning, the two friends met and took a horse-drawn street railway car downtown. They walked to Dearborn Street and easily found the recruiting station. It had once been a small store of some kind, but now there was a large poster on the front window, showing crossed American flags and the words

PRESERVE THE UNION, PROTECT THE CONSTITUTION. ENLIST TODAY IN THE 19TH ILLINOIS VOLUNTEER INFANTRY REGIMENT!

Inside, seated at a desk, was a man in full Zouave uniform with pairs of yellow v-shaped stripes on his sleeves. He gave them a big grin as they entered and introduced himself as Corporal Griggs. Upon being told they had come to enlist, he took them into a small room where they undressed and were examined by a doctor. The doctor thumped their chests, asked them some questions, looked at their tongues, teeth, and fingers.

"They'll do," he called to Corporal Griggs.

Jesse and Harlow signed some papers agreeing to serve in the regiment for three years. With right hands upraised, they swore an oath to defend the government of the United States and the United States Constitution.

"All right, boys, you're in the Army," Corporal Griggs told them. He went through some papers on his desk and consulted one for a moment. "I want you to come back here next Saturday morning at nine o'clock. Don't be late! I'll put you on the train that'll take you to Huntsville, Alabama, where the regiment is encamped." He paused a moment. "You might want to bring a few things with you. A couple of handkerchiefs, maybe; the government don't issue those. Tintypes of your Ma and Pa. Things like that."

The days seemed to creep by until Saturday dawned. Jesse awoke early and hurriedly dressed. He wrote a note to his mother. It said:

Dear Ma,

I have enlisted in the Army, in a good Illinois regiment. Please don't worry, I will be all right.

15

This is something I really want to do very much. I feel it will do me good.

I am with Harlow Basset. We joined together and will look after each other.

I will write to you as soon as I get to where we are going. Please tell Pa I love him. Do not worry. I will be all right.

Your loving son,
Jesse.

He folded it in half and put it on top of his pillow. It was a Saturday, and his mother and father were still in bed. The note would not be found for a long time. He quietly left the house.

He took a street railway car downtown and walked to Dearborn Street. He saw Harlow waiting for him in front of the recruiting station. They entered together.

There were three other young men at the recruiting station, and they, too, were recruits for the 19th Regiment. "Mornin' fellers," said one of them. "Where you from?"

"We live here in Chicago," Harlow told him. "I'm Harlow Basset and this is Jesse Bowman."

"I'm Jim McCabe and this is John Crocker," said McCabe, indicating the man beside him. "We're from Niles." Niles was a little town not far from Chicago. They all exchanged handshakes. McCabe was sandy haired. Crocker was blond. Both men were rather heavyset and full-faced. Jesse thought that the two were probably a few years older than he and Harlow.

The other man came forward, hand extended. "Elisha Graham, Barrington," he said, naming another small town near Chicago. He was small and dark haired, sporting a dark-brown moustache that curled around his mouth down to the edges of his jaw. Jesse thought he was older than the rest of the recruits, maybe in his twenties.

We ought to get to know these fellows, thought Jesse. Looking at McCabe, he said, "Why did you fellows join the army?"

McCabe grinned. "We figured it would have to be a mite better than pitchin' hay all day."

"To see some excitement," said Crocker, nodding.

"I guess that's pretty much why we joined, too," said Jesse, indicating Harlow and himself. He looked toward Graham. "How about you, Elisha?"

"I decided it was time I did something about what I believe in," Graham said. "I'm an abolitionist. I should fight for it!"

Jesse and Harlow made sounds indicating mild approval. Jesse still was not quite sure whether he disapproved of slavery or did not care one way or the other, but he did not want to get into any kind of difference of opinion with someone he had just met.

Corporal Griggs appeared and marched them to the railroad depot. He spoke with a railroad official and then took the five recruits to the boxcar that would be theirs until they reached Huntsville, Alabama. He wished them luck and left. They clambered into the boxcar.

The boxcar was half full with piles of cordwood and stacked wooden boxes with the word HARDTACK stenciled on them. After about half an hour, the recruits felt the train jerk into motion. Jesse's heart pounded with excitement, and he took a shuddering breath. He was in the Army and on his way to the war.

chapter three

Life as a Soldier

The trip lasted about two days with the train making occasional stops. The recruits sat with their backs against the rear wall of the boxcar and stretched out flat on the wooden floor to sleep. They kept the sliding door on the boxcar's side slightly open to let in air and daylight. They watched little country towns slide by, each one much like another.

On the morning of the third day, the train puffed slowly to a stop, and after a time the door on the side of the boxcar was slid fully aside. The railroad track ran right through the town of Huntsville, which was one of the reasons why Union forces had seized the town, and a Union Army encampment had been built with the track running through it. The recruits had reached their destination.

Several soldiers, standing outside, urged them to come out. They did so, and got their first sight of a military camp. "Look at all them tents!" exclaimed John Crocker, and indeed, there were rows upon rows of white tents with v-shaped roofs, and numbers of long, narrow gray-painted wooden buildings.

"First we'll show you where your tent is," said a man with corporal's stripes on his sleeves, "then we'll take you to the quartermaster sergeant for your uniforms and equipment. Come on."

They followed him some distance to a row of tents, and he stopped before one that had "19th Rgt C 6" stenciled across one side in black paint. "Here you are, boys. Nineteenth Regiment, Company C, Tent 6." He pointed to a single exceedingly tall pine tree about twenty feet away. "Use that tree for a landmark to find your way back here. You can see it from most everywhere in camp."

They next followed him to one of the long buildings, where the quartermaster sergeant was located. They entered the building, finding it lined with tables piled high with clothing and many objects they were unfamiliar with. A portly man with the three v-shaped stripes of a sergeant came toward them. "All right, boys, take all your clothes off and pile 'em here." He patted an empty table. "We'll send 'em back to your parents by mail."

He beckoned the boys to follow him to various tables from which he handed them garments. Each recruit received a tan-colored undershirt and pair of ankle-length drawers, a gray flannel shirt, a blue vest, a coat, pair of trousers, a pair of socks, a round, flat-topped cap with a black leather visor, a black leather belt with an oval brass buckle bearing the letters U.S., and a pair of suspenders. They were also given a pair of what were called gaiters. They were lower-leg coverings, made of light-brown canvas, that covered the top of a man's foot and buttoned up the outside of the leg, halfway to the knee. "You tuck the bottoms of your pants legs into these," the sergeant said. "That will keep the bottoms of your pants from gettin' snagged on somethin'. These will get soft and white after they're washed a few times."

Jesse was disappointed. The coat was not a short Zouave-type jacket; it was a thigh-length coat such as ordinary soldiers of the Union Army wore, while the pants were light blue.

"I thought we'd get red pants," he told the sergeant.

The sergeant grinned. "Red pants? They're for parades and such. They're too expensive to give to soldiers that are goin' to be out fightin' in woods and fields. Your cap is red, though, that'll show you're a Zouave."

Jesse and the others then picked out pairs of square-toed black leather shoes for themselves. Jesse was surprised that unlike civilian shoes, which would either fit one foot or the other, each of these was made to fit both left and right feet.

The last item of clothing given to them was a dark-blue greatcoat for winter wear. When completely clothed in his uniform, Jesse was rather uncomfortable. It did not seem to fit very well. The cuffs of his coat sleeves reached halfway down over his hands, the collar was too wide, and his pants were a little too long. He decided, however, that the other recruits looked just as bad.

With the uniform completed, each recruit began to receive what was called "field equipment." The first item was a canvas knapsack. It was coated with baked-on tar to make it waterproof. It was worn on a man's back, held in place with a set of straps that passed over and under his arms and stretched across his chest.

The recruits were then each given a haversack, a canvas bag with a long strap to hang over a shoulder. Like the knapsack, it was waterproofed with a coating of baked-on tar. "This is for your field rations," the sergeant told them. "Three days worth."

Next came two blankets. One was made of heavy brown cotton cloth. The other was also cloth, but was coated on one side with rubber. There was a slit in the middle of this one.

Jesse wondered why.

He and the others stared at what was given them next, unable to decide what it was. It was a square piece of heavy cloth about five feet long on each side, with a row of buttons and a row of buttonholes on three sides and a pair of holes in each corner. The sergeant also gave each man four wooden pegs, flat on one end and pointed on the other. "Put those in your knapsack," he told the men.

"One o' those cloth pieces is called a shelter half," the sergeant continued. "Here's what you can do with two of 'em." He began inserting the buttons on one side of a square into the buttonholes on a side of another. When he finished, he had a rectangle.

"Two men take their muskets, with bayonets on, and stick 'em in the ground as far apart as the width o' this," he told them. "Stretch a rope tight between 'em, by tying the ends o' the rope onto the musket trigger guards. Then put the middle of the cloth over the rope and peg the bottoms hangin' down on each side by putting a peg through the hole in each corner and poundin' 'em into the ground. That gives two men a tent to sleep in. Old soldiers call 'em 'pup tents,' because they say they're only big enough for a little dog. But they'll keep the rain off your head."

They now received a leather box called a cartridge-box that hung by a strap from the left shoulder to the right hip, and a small leather pouch called a cap box that could be attached to the belt. None of the recruits knew what either a cartridge or a cap was, but the sergeant assured them they would find out.

They were then given a large cup, a plate, and a knife and fork, all made out of thick tin. Jesse was beginning to think that the things being issued would never come to an end, but the last item, a canteen, was finally provided. It was made of tin and covered with dark-blue cloth, with a white cloth strap for hanging it on one's shoulder.

"Put your shelter half and greatcoat in your knapsack," the sergeant instructed them. "Put your cup and plate and knife and fork in there too. Roll up your blankets inside each other and fasten the roll on top of the knapsack with the straps there. Put the knapsack on. Clip your cap pouch on your belt." He then told them to return to their tent.

As Jesse trudged to his tent, with his heavy knapsack and blanket roll on his back and his canteen bouncing against his hip, he grunted to himself, "I feel like a danged pack mule!"

When the five recruits reached their tent and went in, they found several other soldiers inside, seated on logs. These were older men; one looked as if he might be as much as forty.

"New recruits, eh?" said one, eyeing them. "Welcome to Company C o' the Nineteenth. This is where ye'll eat, sleep, and live, until we get orders to march."

Elisha Graham looked around. "Where do we sleep? I don't see any beds."

The man grinned. "See them logs piled in the corner there? And see all that straw piled next to 'em? You bunches some straw together and that's your mattress. Then you puts a log on each side o' you, so you won't roll out o' bed while you're sleepin'."

"You'd better stow your equipment out of the way," one of the other soldiers said. "Fix up your beds where you want 'em and put your knapsack and haversack on top of 'em. By the way, my name is Calvin Martin. I'm from Waukegan." Waukegan was a northern Illinois town near Chicago. Jesse suspected that with the 19th being an Illinois regiment, most of the men in it were probably from the state it was named after.

Near noontime, a short bouncy bugle call sounded from various parts of the camp. "That's the mess call," Calvin said. "Let's go have dinner. Bring your cups and plates." When he put on his uniform coat, they saw that he had corporal's stripes on his sleeves. When he saw that they had noticed this, he smiled and said, "I'm the corporal of your section. There's a full twelve of us, now you're here."

The recruits found that the men of each tent stood in line to get their food. Beans from iron pots hanging over an open fire were ladled out to each man as he got to the front of the line. The rest of dinner consisted of very strong coffee and very hard, dry biscuits called hardtack, which most soldiers dunked into their coffee. They took dinner back to the tent and ate sitting on logs.

That night, as the recruits started to undress for bed, one of the older soldiers who had been on campaigns told them to sleep in their clothes and just take their shoes off. "That way, if there's an attack, you won't have to be fightin' half naked," the man said.

The day began at sunrise, with a long bugle call that the older soldiers called by a word that sounded like "revuhlee." They said it was a French word, but no one knew what it meant. They informed Jesse that there were lyrics to it that went, "You can't get 'em up, you can't get 'em up, you can't get 'em up, in the mor-ning."

Jesse joined the rest of the company in a formation of three long lines of men. This was called "falling in." A sergeant then did the "roll call," which was a calling of the names of everyone in the company, in alphabetical order. When a man's name was called, he was expected to answer by yelling "here!" The roll call was done, Jesse learned from Corporal Martin, to see if anyone had deserted during the night or previous day.

After the roll call came a brief period of drilling, called "short drill," that lasted one hour. However, while the entire company drilled together, the recruits, who knew nothing at all of drilling, were taken to one side, formed into what was called the "Awkward Squad," and taught the basics. The first thing was to learn to march in step. This was done by what was called Zouave cadence, which consisted of loudly counting all together, on each eight steps taken, over and over—"One, two, three, four, five, six, seven, TIGER!" When that was mastered, the recruits were taught to obey commands while marching. This consisted mainly of doing the right thing when given such commands as "Column Right—March, To the Left Flank—March, To the Rear—March" without going the wrong way or tripping over one's own feet.

Then came breakfast, which was coffee, hardtack, and fried bacon.

After breakfast, Jesse and the other recruits were given their first lesson in how to use a musket. They were each given a musket, a bayonet in a scabbard, a number of cartridges to put in their cartridge boxes, and a number of caps to put in their cap boxes. A cartridge was a bullet wrapped in a paper tube containing a small amount of gunpowder. The cartridge box held forty cartridges. The caps, officially called percussion caps, were tiny cups of thin copper filled with an explosive substance that would go off when the cap was sharply struck.

A burly sergeant took the recruits out to the edge of an empty weed-covered field and showed them how to load and fire. "You take a cartridge out o' your box," he told them, doing so. "You bite the ball out o' the cartridge and hold it in your mouth." He did this with a quick jerk of his head. "Don't swaller it!" he said. Several of the recruits chuckled. Talking out of the corner of his mouth, he continued, "Then you pour the powder out o' the cartridge into your musket barrel." With the butt of his musket resting on the ground and the muzzle pointing straight up, he emptied the contents of the paper into the muzzle. "Throw the empty cartridge away," he told them, crumpling it into a loose ball and giving it a toss. Then he put his hand up to his mouth and spat the bullet into it. "Now, you put the bullet in. Be sure the pointed end is facin' outwards, so it comes out first." He put the bullet into the muzzle.

In the wooden stock of the musket, beneath the barrel, was a long groove in which the ramrod was sheathed—a metal rod as long as the musket barrel, with a knob on the end. Grasping the knob, the sergeant slid the ramrod out of its resting place. "Now you've got to ram it down good." Inserting the rod into the barrel, he vigorously pumped his arm up and down several times.

Sliding the ramrod out of the musket, he looked up at the recruits and shook it at them. "You've got to always remember," he said, forcefully, "to take the ramrod out. Some fellers forget, and then they *shoot* it out, and it's *gone*. If that happens, you might as well throw your musket away, because you can't load it without a ramrod, and an unloaded musket is no help if there's rebels comin' at you!"

Jesse and the other recruits eyed him solemnly. *I've got to remember that*, Jesse told himself.

The sergeant slid the ramrod back into its socket. "Next," he said, "you've got to cock it." He grasped the hammerlike device jutting up on the musket's side, above the trigger, and yanked it back with a clacking sound. Then he reached into the pouch on his belt and took out a percussion cap. "After it's cocked, you put a cap in." He moved close to the recruits, stepping in front of each one, to show him where the cap was inserted.

Stepping away from them, he said, "Now, she's ready to shoot. When you pull the trigger, the hammer jumps forward and hits the cap. That makes the cap explode, and the cap explosion makes the powder in the barrel explode, and that shoots the ball out." He lifted the musket to his shoulder and pulled the trigger. There was a loud bang and a huge spurt of white smoke from the musket's muzzle. Jesse, who had never heard a firearm go off, could not keep his body from making a startled twitch.

Jesse and the others found that the vast, sprawling encampment that was now their home was actually the camp of the Army of the Ohio, commanded by a general by the name of Don Carlos Buell. The army was divided into three units called corps, each of which was made up of three divisions, which were each composed of three units called brigades. A brigade was formed of four regiments. Jesse's regiment was in the Eighth Brigade, of the Third Division, in the I Corps.

Jesse learned that his regiment was commanded by a colonel who was a former Russian army officer named Ivan Vasilevich Turchin, who had changed his name to John Basil Turchin. He was a large man with a high forehead, and jet-black hair, a short beard, and a bushy moustache. He was also the commander of the army's Eighth Brigade, which was made up of the 19th and 24th Illinois Regiments, 18th Ohio Regiment, and 37th Indiana Regiment.

Corporal Martin told the recruits that Colonel Turchin had fought against French troops in Europe and had seen French Zouave troops in action. He had been tremendously impressed by them and when he had been put in command of the Chicago Zouaves. He had determined to teach them French Zouave fighting methods. "You'll learn to fight like those Frenchies," Martin told Jesse and the others with a grin.

He was right. Jesse soon found his company practicing what the captain told them was called the Zouave Rush. It made use of speed, concealment, and rapid fire. Instead of trotting forward in formation and pausing to fire once or twice, as was the usual way for an American force to charge, Jesse's company practiced rushing forward at top speed widely spread out, which made them harder to shoot at. Jesse learned to suddenly drop flat to the ground during his rush, rise up to his knees to fire a shot, fling himself to the ground again and reload, lying flat. Then he would spring up and continue his forward rush. The captain explained that this had the effect of confusing the enemy's fire—a man would take aim at a running figure that suddenly vanished from sight into the tall grass or underbrush. The speed of the charge, and the popping up and down of many figures among those making the charge also had a nerve-wracking effect.

Jesse and the other members of the 19th Regiment were proud of themselves and felt their regiment was something special. Corporal Martin and the other noncommissioned officers were constantly reminding the men of this. "Never forget," Martin told Jesse and the others, "you're in the best regiment, of the best brigade, of the best division, of the best corps, in the army. That'll help you fight harder!"

In the encampment there were a number of Northern civilian men who had small businesses and were allowed to sell things to soldiers. They were known as sutlers. Jesse bought a pencil, some paper, and envelopes, and wrote a letter to his parents, telling them how they could get in touch with him. He asked them to forgive him for

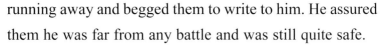

running away and begged them to write to him. He assured them he was far from any battle and was still quite safe.

However, he soon found that he might not be as safe as he thought. Although the region of Alabama where Huntsville was located was occupied by the Union Army, there were small units of Confederate soldiers moving about in it, doing whatever they could to cause trouble for Union troops. On the first of May, Jesse and the other recruits were shocked to see soldiers of one of the brigade's regiments, the 18th Ohio, streaming into the camp looking as if they had been in a battle. One of the regiment's supply wagons carried bloody, wounded men, and another wagon contained a number of bloody dead men. Jesse and Harlow rushed up to one of the Ohio soldiers. "What's happened?" Harlow asked breathlessly.

"We was marchin' through that little town called Athens, a few miles from here," the man replied. "All of a sudden, there was rebel soldiers shootin' at us from the windows of houses along the streets! We took around thirty-four, thirty-five casualties. The colonel took us out o' there on the double, but we had to leave most of our supply wagons behind. The rebels got 'em now." He paused for a moment, then said, bitterly, "There was some of the town folk shootin' at us along with the reb soldiers—some of the men."

"That's against the rules of war," said a sergeant who had come up behind him. "Colonel Turchin will give 'em hell for doing that!"

He was right. When the colonel of the 18th Ohio made his report to Colonel Turchin about what had happened, Turchin became enraged. It was rumored that he had shouted, in his Russian accent, "Is against laws of war! We shall teach them lesson!"

chapter four

On Guard in a Southern Town

The next morning, Jesse's regiment and the 24th Illinois, another of the 8th Brigade's regiments, were put under marching orders. With a grim-looking Colonel Turchin riding at the head of the column, they marched to the outskirts of Athens, where they were halted. A wagon had accompanied the column, and at a word from Turchin, some soldiers took a tent out of it and began to set it up.

Jesse was not at all sure what was going to happen. He thought there might be a battle or at least some shooting. Some men of the 18th Ohio had certainly been shot in this town, by both Confederate soldiers and men of the town. Maybe they were just waiting for the Illinois boys to show up. Jesse licked his lips nervously. *We'll just have to see what happens*, he decided.

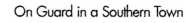

The two infantry regiments had been put into position facing each other across a distance of about fifteen yards. Turchin came pacing between them and halted. In a loud voice he announced in broken English, "I my eyes will shut for two hours. For two hours I will nothing see." Then he gave the command. "Parade—DISMISSED!" He walked to the tent with his arms folded and went inside.

"What does he mean?" Harlow asked Jesse in a low whisper.

"He means he won't be watching us for two hours," came Corporal Martin's voice from behind them. "He's giving us two hours to punish the town."

"All right, boys," said Captain Howard, the commander of Company C, which was Jesse's company. "Just remember, we don't want anybody killed, unless it's a rebel soldier, for sure, and we don't want any houses burnt!"

Some men began to eagerly run into the town; others took their time as if they were heading to a county fair. Jesse, Harlow, and George Walker, a man who had been in the company before they arrived, formed a little group and proceeded cautiously. Jesse looked around for McCabe and Crocker but did not see them or Elisha Graham.

"What are we supposed to do?" wondered Harlow. Walker gave him an odd look.

"Well," said Jesse, "maybe we're supposed to make a lot of noise to get folks scared and worried. Maybe we could yell insults to embarrass 'em. Like, 'Anybody who would vote for Jeff Davis is a jackass!'"

"I think we're supposed to break things," Walker said.

As they moved deeper into Athens and saw what many other soldiers were doing, they became quiet. The streets were filled with active blue-uniformed figures. Men were coming out of houses carrying things—frying pans, pillows, blankets, stools, and various other objects that clearly looked to be of value.

"They're robbing houses!" Jesse exclaimed. As the son of a lawyer, he had been reared to respect law and order, and was shocked by such open defiance toward it.

Two soldiers came out of a house and were followed out by a middle-aged man in civilian clothing who was cursing them, fiercely. One of the soldiers turned, and with a vicious swing of his fist, hit the man in the face, knocking him back through the doorway.

"They're beating folks!" said Harlow.

"Well, he was just a no-account secesher," George said, using a Northerner's term for citizens of states that had seceded. "He might even have been one of those that helped the rebel soldiers shoot at our boys."

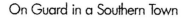

Continuing to walk, they went past a store. Soldiers were coming out of it with bags of flour, boxes of crackers, and armloads of cans. One young soldier carried a large smoked ham.

"Maybe we could do a little o' that," suggested George.

"My pa owns a dry-goods store," said Harlow softly. "That's how he makes a living. The folks that own this store will have a troubled time if all their stock is stolen."

"Serve 'em right," muttered George.

They passed a man lying in the street. He was another middle-aged man, obviously one of the townspeople. He was alive, but unconscious. There was blood on his head. Jesse thought he must have been hit with a musket butt.

As they were passing a large home, a woman began to scream inside. "No, no, no!" She sounded desperate and terrified. They saw that the front door was hanging ajar, as if it had been forced open. The three of them stopped dead, staring at it.

"Maybe we should—help her," Harlow said, but George grabbed him by the arm.

"No! Let's just get out o' here!" said George.

"I want to get all the way out," Jesse snarled. "I'm leaving!"

"The two hours ain't up yet," George said.

"I don't care. I'm going."

"I'll go with you, Jess," Harlow said quietly.

"I'm stayin,'" George said, folding his arms defiantly.

Jesse and Harlow turned away from him without a word and began to walk back through the town. There were fewer soldiers in sight now, many of them having moved farther on into the town. There were no townspeople in sight, but Jesse caught a flash of a woman's face glaring through an upstairs window. "Let's move faster," he suggested. "If any of these folks have guns, they might take a shot at us for what's been done to them."

Harlow nodded, and they picked up their pace. They walked in silence for a time, then Jesse spoke. "You know, I never imagined anything like this, Harlow. I never dreamed a war could cause things like this to happen to ordinary folks that weren't soldiers. I never imagined that *our* soldiers could do things like this—rob people, and beat people, and . . . mistreat womenfolk!"

Several days later, the whole army was notified that attacks against civilians and damage to civilian property by soldiers were regarded as crimes by the United States Army and would be punished. General Buell relieved Colonel Turchin of command and replaced him with Brigadier General James Negley. Buell began a program of guarding the homes and fields of prosperous Southern citizens who might be targets for robbery and damage by Northern soldiers.

Jesse heard many of his fellow soldiers grumbling about this. A number of the larger and more wealthy looking houses had no men in them, and the Union soldiers suspected that was because the men were away serving in the Confederate Army. The soldiers could see no reason for guarding the property of men who were their enemies and were fighting against them. Jim McCabe confided to Jesse, "It doesn't make sense to me, to have to look after the houses of families that may have sons, or even a father, who's in the rebel army trying to kill us!" A tall, gangly soldier named Cyrus Bolton, in Jesse's section, was often heard to snarl, "We oughter just *burn* the damn houses, then we wouldn't have to set anybody to guardin' 'em!" Cyrus had straw-colored hair, pale gray eyes, and a homely but pleasant face, except when he was complaining about rebels.

General Buell also took steps to protect Southerners from the soldiers' tendency to forage—pick up food from farm fields, orchards, and forests owned by Southerners. "Foraging is really just stealing, you know," Jesse pointed out to Harlow, "but sometimes it's the only way to keep from being hungry when the rations they give us just aren't enough. It's the army's fault, dang it!" Nevertheless, Buell punished foraging severely. A man of a regiment in Jesse's brigade was hung from a tree branch by his thumbs for six hours for picking two ears of corn out of a cornfield.

However, there were ways for clever and imaginative soldiers to get around punishments for foraging, and Jesse was lucky enough to fall in with such a group from his company. The regiment had been on short rations for several days and Jesse's breakfast had been one piece of hardtack. He was hungry enough to accept anything his companions could think of to gain some food for themselves.

Moving through a patch of woods, they encountered a large hog. It was quite tame and obviously belonged to some Southerner living nearby. Someone's musket happened to "accidentally" go off, as sometimes actually happened, and the bullet buried itself in the animal's head, killing it instantly. The man who shot the hog had been a butcher at the Chicago stockyards. He cut off the hog's head and hooves and skinned it, burying everything in six different places. Then the men carried the carcass back to camp and proudly showed it off as a "wild bear" they had encountered in the woods. The captain looked at it, but could not tell what kind of animal it had been, so he accepted their word. That night, Jesse and his friends happily dined on what they called "roast porkbear."

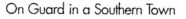

In time, it became Jesse's turn to go on guard duty. He and seven other men of his company were put to patrolling the grounds of a stately home some distance from Huntsville. It was surrounded by broad fields where various kinds of crops were growing, tended by black people that Jesse figured might be slaves. He noticed that the inhabitants of the house were all women: an elderly lady, two middle-aged women, and a young girl about his age. The girl was quite pretty, Jesse thought.

Each of the soldiers was given a portion of the grounds to watch, known as a "post." They were armed with loaded muskets with bayonets attached and under orders to march back and forth with musket on shoulder, the position known as right-shoulder arms. Each post had a number, and if a man saw something wrong, he was to call out the number, and the commander of the group, known as the corporal of the guard, would come running.

However, about midway through the day, all these orders and regulations vanished from Jesse's mind when he was sure he heard a muffled shriek. He raced toward the place he thought it came from, where there was a small grove of trees. Thrusting his way among them, he was horrified to see the young Southern girl struggling with one of the soldiers of Jesse's company, a man named Dickinson. Instantly, memory of the woman he had heard

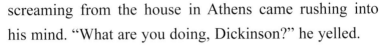

screaming from the house in Athens came rushing into his mind. "What are you doing, Dickinson?" he yelled.

"Git outta here, Bowman," Dickinson snarled at him.

"Let go of her!" Jesse demanded, advancing toward him. Dickinson was several years older and a bit taller, but Jesse was heavier and was moving with a determined look on his face. The older boy took a step backward and the girl was able to whirl herself out of his grasp. With a quick glance at Jesse, she fled.

Dickinson glared at Jesse and swore at him. Jesse placed his musket on the ground—he wanted no accidents—then charged straight at the other man. Dickinson stared at him with his mouth open, backing away with his hands up in front of his face. Jesse swung a roundhouse punch that caught Dickinson on the cheek with a meaty smack and knocked him onto his back.

Jesse was a little surprised by the effectiveness of his blow but decided to make the most of it. He folded his arms across his chest and glared down at the man. "Had enough or do you need more?"

Dickinson was rubbing his cheek. "I'm licked, Bowman."

Jesse relaxed. "All right, then. I'm just going to tell you that if I see or hear of you trying to force yourself on any girl again, you'll find yourself in a real muss, I vow." He pointed a finger. "If I was to report you to the corporal

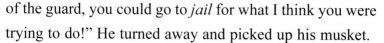

of the guard, you could go to *jail* for what I think you were trying to do!" He turned away and picked up his musket.

Several days later, Jesse again drew guard duty at the house where he had punched Dickinson, although Jesse's post today was on a different section of the grounds. About midway through the morning, he noticed that someone was approaching him, and was pleasantly surprised to see that it was the young girl from the house. He was even happier to see that she was directly approaching him, rather than merely passing by. He halted his pacing, and waited.

She stopped some distance away. It seemed to him that she was somewhat nervous. After a few moments she spoke, in what struck Jesse's ears as a charming Southern accent.

"Sir, I want to thank you for coming to my assistance a few days ago. I am glad to know that not all Yankees are villains."

He had to clear his throat before answering; he was also somewhat nervous. He had never been very confident around girls and did not really know any too well. "I assure you, Ma'am, that most Yankees are not villains. Most Yankee soldiers would have done just what I did, as a matter of honor."

"Well, that is good to know," she said. "We hear some dreadful stories about things Yankees have done." She hesitated for a moment and then blurted out a question in a rush of words. "Why are you-all down here, anyway?"

Jesse did not understand her at first; then he realized she was asking why a Union army was in the South. He was not quite sure how to answer, then decided to fall back on the reason that was commonly used in the North to explain the war. "To preserve the Union," he told her.

She frowned slightly. "You mean make things like they were before the secession? We can't allow that. Your government wants to take away our property."

Now Jesse frowned, uncertain of what she was talking about. "I've never heard a word about taking away people's homes or farms," he protested. "I don't think—"

"No, no," she interrupted. "I mean our Negroes."

Jesse was stunned. He had never given any thought to how people in the South might regard their slaves. He had always just thought of slaves as being a kind of unpaid servant. But—*property*?

"Property is houses and farms and goods," he said slowly. "I don't think a *person* can be property!"

She looked at him in a way that made him feel foolish or stupid. "Why, we *own* them," she told him. "Of course they're our property."

He did not know what to say next, but he was saved from having to say anything. There was a call from the plantation.

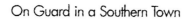

"Becky?"

"That's Granny," the girl said. "She probably thinks I shouldn't be talking to a Yankee. I have to go."

"Your name's Rebecca?" he asked.

She nodded. "Rebecca Harrison. You can call me Becky. And what's your name, Yankee boy?"

"Jesse Bowman. Private Jesse Bowman."

She nodded, then turned and dashed toward the house. Jesse watched her go. She had given him a lot to think about. There were apparently great differences he had not been aware of in the ways Northerners and Southerners regarded things. He thought he understood better, now, how the war had come about.

He very much wanted to talk with her again. When he went off guard duty and returned to camp, he went to the tent that served as an office for his company's first sergeant. The first sergeant was the man who assigned guard duty sites.

"I say, sergeant, when my turn comes for guard duty again, could you send me back to the Harrison place?"

"Sure, Bowman. It don't matter who goes where. Something you like out there?"

"I guess you might say so," Jesse said.

It was a week before he drew guard duty again, and he was delighted to find that the first sergeant had obligingly assigned him to Becky's house. Of course, he realized that she might not want to talk to him again, but he hoped she would.

His hopes came true. In the early afternoon, she emerged, rather furtively, from a bushy area. "I saw you from an upstairs window," she told him. "I'm not supposed to talk to Yankee soldiers, of course, but since we've already talked once, I don't see how it can matter."

She was very interested about his life in the North, and what it was like to live in a big city like Chicago. She asked him if he had been in any battles yet.

"Not yet," he told her, "but I'm sure I will be. I'll be in the army for three years."

"Oh, the war will be over long before then, Jesse," she assured him. "I'm sorry, but the South is going to win."

He wanted to tell her she was wrong, but decided the last thing he wanted to do was to get into an argument with her. He changed the subject.

After a time, she said, "I'd better go. Somebody might see us and then I wouldn't ever be able to talk to you again." She turned away, then turned back again. She put a hand on his arm and said, seriously, "If you do have to fight in a battle, Jesse, I surely hope you won't be hurt." She rustled into the bushes and was gone.

Jesse had the definite feeling that Becky had quickly become quite fond of him. It was a feeling that made him very happy. He began to consider the possibility that

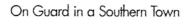

sometime in the future she might be willing to keep company with him. They could go on picnics together and things of that sort. He also began to wonder if she might ever want to do some "sparking"—hugging and kissing—with him.

However, two mornings later, the captain commanding his company called the men together and told them to start making preparations to leave on a long march southward the next morning. Jesse saw there would be no way to notify Becky about this, no way to even say good-bye. He knew he would be unable to slip out of camp, because guards would be posted everywhere to prevent men from deserting. He realized he would probably never even see her again, and he found himself regretting this as he got his gear together for the long march south.

chapter five

A Long March

When the command to "fall in," was given the next morning, the main thing on Jesse Bowman's mind was, "Where are we going?"

He soon found out that the march was the beginning of General Buell's long-planned invasion of eastern Tennessee. This information quickly leaked down from the top commanders to the rank-and-file soldiers. They were going into eastern Tennessee to conquer it for the Union.

Eastern Tennessee was under the control of a Confederate army known as the Army of Tennessee, commanded by a general named Braxton Bragg. Jesse and everyone else felt sure there would someday be a battle with this army. *Well,* Jesse told himself, *this is why you enlisted.*

After breakfast, the army began to "form up" for the march. Each man was issued eighty cartridges and eight days worth of field rations. However, the cartridge box would hold only forty cartridges and the haversack held only three days worth of rations. The forty extra cartridges and five days of field rations had to go somewhere, and Jesse decided the only place he had for them was the knapsack, so into the knapsack they went. This made it considerably heavier, and as it already contained a shelter half, a greatcoat, an extra shirt, a pair of drawers, a pair of socks, his eating utensils, and eight tent pegs. He once again felt like an overloaded pack mule.

It took a long time to get everything ready, but finally the command to "Forward—MARCH" began to move down the brigades, and the men began to step off. Jesse found that he was immensely happy—despite the loss of Becky. He was going on what was called a campaign. He was almost certain to see battle, where he could prove himself.

Everyone seemed happy. Jesse glanced to his right where Harlow was marching next to him, and saw that the usually serious Harlow had a wide smile on his face. Looking about, Jesse noticed that many of the men were smiling. There was a steady murmur of conversation, accompanied by the steady tramp of feet and occasional bursts of laughter.

After about an hour had passed, Jesse noticed that men were throwing things away. The most common objects seemed to be cast-iron frying pans, cast-iron pots, and small axes. These were things men had brought along, stuck through or slung from their belts, to make camping easier. Now, they were trying to lighten their loads, Jesse understood, and were dispensing with what they felt they could do without.

When the sun was just about directly overhead, the march was halted for a midday meal. Some men from each company went out to gather firewood; others went to secure water. Their commanders always made sure there was a creek, stream, or river nearby. After a suitable time, the march resumed.

Near sundown, the march was halted for the night. Each regiment put a number of soldiers known as "pickets" out in position around the area it occupied to guard against the approach of an enemy force. Once again, men went out for wood and water, while others assembled shelter halves into tents. Jesse and Harlow had agreed to share shelter halves. The tents were loosely arranged in a circle, and when the wood-gatherers brought their loads of branches, they piled some of them in the middle of the circle to make a cooking fire. The fire was lit with one of the wooden matches they all carried in their pockets. Chunks of salt pork from their haversacks were stuck on long peeled branches that were then pushed into the ground to hang over the fire. The meat was eaten with pieces of hardtack. The coffee was boiled in an iron pot that sat right on the fire. It was sweetened in the cup from a small bag of sugar that had been included with the field rations. Jesse noticed that many men had mixed their coffee and sugar rations together, which gave them one less thing to carry.

After eating, a number of men went to bathe in the nearby creek. There was an army regulation about keeping clean, but it was difficult, and some men paid little attention to it.

In the morning, breakfast of coffee, hardtack, and bacon were made in the same fashion the supper had been. The tents were taken apart, and the shelter halves put back into knapsacks. The roll was called. The march resumed.

After a number of days of steady marching, Jesse discovered that his uniform was beginning to come apart. It appeared that some pieces of his clothing were made of the cheapest, flimsiest material there was, and the strain of continuous daily movement was too much for it. His socks were virtually rags, his shirt was coming to pieces, and the sleeves were coming off his coat. His shoes were coming apart, too. The heels were worn down to stubs, and the soles were getting holes in them.

Jesse was not the only soldier with such problems. Every man in the company was having them. Harlow told Jesse that his socks had turned into tatters, and he had simply thrown them away. His feet were bare inside his shoes. His shoes, like Jesse's, were also coming apart.

Some men had special problems. "The seat o' my pants is wearin' out," complained Cyrus Bolton. "Pretty soon, I ain't goin' to be fit to be seen!"

Blankets seemed particularly flimsy. They were wearing away. The nights were cool and most men were taking the blanket rolls off their knapsacks and unrolling them to sleep under. In the morning they had to be rolled up again. A few days of such handling and the blankets were threadbare and full of holes.

"Somebody has to do something," Harlow said as he, Jesse, and others sat around their campfire after a day's march. "We'll be marching naked pretty soon! Somebody has to talk to the first sergeant and get him to talk to the lieutenant or the captain."

Corporal Martin sighed. "I can tell you for sure, Basset, that the lieutenant, the captain, and even the colonel know all about this. This isn't anything unusual and it isn't just happening to you fellows in this regiment. It's happening all through the brigade, all through the division, and all through the army. It's the way things are. Uniforms wear out fast on a march. I knew a soldier from another regiment once who told me the regiment started out on a campaign with brand-new uniforms, and within two weeks, all the uniforms were comin' apart and half the men were marchin' barefoot!"

"The government must be buying the cheapest clothes they can find," Jesse cried out in outrage.

"Oh, that's not the way of it, Bowman," the corporal assured him. "Believe me, the government's probably payin' the highest prices for everything. It's the manufacturers. They're usin' the cheapest goods they can find and chargin' the highest prices they can get. They're getting rich off this war. It's a rich man's war and a poor man's fight, Bowman."

The corporal took a sip from his cup of coffee. "I can tell you this, Basset. I had a talk with the first sergeant and, like I said, the colonel knows all about this. He's been doing everything he could to take care of it. He's had riders and wagons goin' around for days, getting what they can. There are other regiments that are a lot better off than we are, with stuff to spare, and there's a big shipment of supplies comin' down from Kentucky. I can promise you that in a few more days, you'll get replacements for just about everything you need."

He was as good as his word. Several days later, during the midday halt, wagons came rumbling through the area occupied by the 19th Regiment. They were piled high with supplies of all kinds. With whoops and catcalls, men came rushing at them from all directions, in a mad scramble to get as much as they could. Jesse managed to put together a pair of shoes that more or less fit him, snatched up a coat that was only a bit too big, and secured two blankets that appeared to be rather well made. Later, he traded one of the blankets for a shirt.

July slid into August and still the army trudged on. The heat was severe, and Jesse found himself suffering in his heavy wool clothing. The dust kicked up from the road by many thousands of marching feet crept in at the neck and wrists of his shirt and mixed with perspiration to form an itching, stinging body coating. Jesse, like all the others, simply endured it.

One morning there was a surprise. As the soldiers began to form up into their marching order, there was a stirring in the ranks. The army had camped at a crossroad the night before, and as the march began, it became clear it was turning onto the adjoining road. "We're changing direction!" Harlow said.

"Maybe its just a shortcut," Jesse suggested.

"I don't think so, Jess." Harlow pointed. "That piece of land was directly ahead of us yesterday, and now it's to our right. We're moving away from it instead of toward it!"

Elisha Graham, who was on Jesse's other side in the column, was nodding. "I do believe you're right, Harlow."

As days went on, the change of direction became more obvious. Finally, the answer to what was going on leaked down to the lower ranks of the army. Instead of continuing southward they were now swinging around to head northward, toward the state of Kentucky. It had been learned that the Confederate army General Buell had been trying to find in eastern Tennessee was now moving to invade Kentucky, a Union state, and General Buell had been ordered to prevent this.

Another morning came and the army began to form up for the march. Everyone knew that Buell was taking the army to Louisville, the biggest city in Kentucky, where reinforcements were waiting. But it quickly became obvious that today something was different. The brigade the 19th Illinois was in was faced in a different direction.

"What's going on?" wondered Harlow.

"Looks to me like we may not be going with the rest of the army," Jesse offered. "Here comes the general, I think he's going to tell us what's going on."

Brigadier General Negley rode to the middle of the formation and stopped. "Soldiers," he called loudly. "We are being reassigned. We are being sent to Nashville, Tennessee, where we will be protecting the Army of the Ohio's rear from attack." He backed his horse up a few paces and gave a command. "Brigade, forward—MARCH!"

Well, here we go back into Tennessee, thought Jesse as he stepped off. They marched for several days and reached Nashville on the fifth of September. Jesse and all the others were delighted to find that there were walled tents available to them that twenty men could share. It was much like being back in camp at Huntsville. They could sleep in comfort instead of in a pup tent. However, they now began a routine of guard duty, picket duty, and periods of drilling they had to endure, and the rations were often far too short.

In late September, the brigade received some interesting news. The commanders of each company had their men assembled and announced that on September 22, President Lincoln had signed what was being called the Emancipation Proclamation. The captains explained that this was a statement that all slaves living in a state that was in rebellion against the United States government, except areas of those states now occupied by Union forces, would be declared free on January 1, 1863.

This news became the subject of much conversation throughout the army. Jesse and the other men of his section talked about it after supper on the day they were told of it.

"What does ee-mansuh-pay-shun *mean*, anyway?" asked Cyrus Bolton.

"To be set free," said Elisha Graham. "I think it's wonderful! God Bless Old Abe!" Elisha was a preacher's son and kept reminding the other soldiers that he was an abolitionist and believed that slavery was an evil created by Satan.

"This law may make the rebels fight harder, though," Jesse said. "They think the slaves are their property." He was thinking of his conversation with Becky. "People will fight if they think somebody is trying to take their property away."

"What will the slaves do if they're set free?" wondered Jim McCabe. "Will they come North?" He said this in a way that made Jesse feel he found it upsetting.

"Some may come North," Corporal Martin said. "What's it matter? There's black folks in the North, now."

McCabe grunted, sullenly.

"It don't matter to me," John Crocker announced. "Whether they go free or stay slaves, I don't care."

"I think it's a good thing," Harlow said quietly.

It seemed to Jesse, as the group began breaking up and heading for tents, that some men were in favor of what the president had done, others were against it, and some had no opinion about it. It was probably that way throughout the whole regiment, he thought, throughout the whole army. As for him, he decided that he was for it. It seemed to him a rather grand thing for the United States to announce it was fighting to make people free.

The days dragged by. Then, on October 10, 1862, a rider came galloping into the town and went straight to the building occupied by General Negley. Within another day, every soldier of the Army of the Ohio in Nashville knew that General Buell and General Bragg had fought a bitter and bloody battle on October 8, at Perryville, Kentucky. The Union Army was still in place and the Confederate Army had withdrawn, so it was a Union victory, but apparently the casualties had been terrible.

"If what they're saying is right, I guess we're lucky to have been here, Jess," Harlow said at supper that night.

"I reckon," Jesse agreed. However, within himself, he still wondered what it would be like to be in a battle and how he would stand up to it.

In the last week of October, word began to spread through the army that Buell had been removed as commander of the Army of the Ohio, and a general named William S. Rosecrans had been appointed commander.

No one seemed to know anything about General Rosecrans, but when he showed up in Kentucky, things began to happen quickly. Within days, the Army of the

Ohio was marching south, back into Tennessee, where it encamped at Nashville.

In mid-November, it was announced that the Army of the Ohio was now officially the XIV Army Corps, and would be known as the Army of the Cumberland. General Rosecrans then began a reorganization of the army, and Jesse soon found himself in General James Negley's Division of General George Thomas's Corps. His brigade was now the Second, which included the 18th and 69th Ohio and 11th Michigan regiments as well as the 19th Illinois regiment.

Things began to get better with Rosecrans in command—in particular, the food. Pickles, pepper, and potatoes, which the soldiers had not seen in months, began to appear in the rations. The pay was provided more regularly, and even the mail was delivered more often. These were things of great importance to a soldier. The men of the Army of the Cumberland decided Rosecrans was the best commander they had ever had. He had become affectionately known throughout the army as "Old Rosy." Jesse was especially pleased by the improved mail delivery. He had written to his parents soon after reaching Nashville and told them how to get in touch with him, and he was now getting letters at least once a week. His parents often let him know how proud they were that he was in the army, and that they were not angry at him for having run away to enlist. However, they also let him know that they missed him very much.

The Confederate Army of Tennessee was also back in Tennessee, and near the end of December, General Rosecrans apparently felt he was ready to search for it and force it into battle. On the morning of Christmas Day, the Army of the Cumberland was ordered to prepare for a march beginning the next day.

Jesse decided to write his parents a Christmas letter, but that made him start thinking about past Christmases at home that had been so different from the Christmas he was experiencing now. He wondered where he might be next Christmas, and what he might be doing. Would he still be in the army, in some other part of the country? Would he still be alive?

The day after Christmas dawned with a sky the color of lead, out of which rain was pouring. Jesse's equipment was piled by his bed. He reached into his haversack and took out his morning rations, two pieces of hardtack and a chunk of raw bacon. Then he opened the flap on his knapsack and rummaged about until he located the blanket that was coated with rubber on one side. He pulled it out and set it aside.

He had learned that it was called a poncho, and it was a rainproof garment for keeping his body from getting wet. He had also learned why there was a slit in its middle. He strapped the knapsack on and slung his canteen and haversack from his shoulders. Then he picked up the poncho, which was rolled up. He shook it open and put his head through the slit. The poncho settled onto his shoulders and hung around him, rubber side out, to about halfway down his legs. Putting on his cap, he pulled it down onto his head as far as he could. He began to gnaw on the raw bacon and hardtack.

When "fall in" was ordered, Jesse had his musket beneath the poncho, cradled in his arm, pointing downward. When the command to march was given, he stepped forward, and with raindrops spattering on his cap, he began to slog miserably along through the thick, ankle-deep mud of the road.

When General Rosecrans ordered the march halted for the night, Jesse and Harlow assembled their tent, grateful for the shelter it would give them from the falling rain. Of course, the ground the tent enclosed was a mass of wet mud, but the two friends had learned from the old soldiers what to do about that. They slipped out of their ponchos and spread them on the ground, rubber side down. The insides of the ponchos were dry, so the two soldiers each had a dry place to sit or lie on.

"This isn't too bad," Jesse said, seating himself. "I'm surely glad we didn't get picket duty!"

"Me too," Harlow agreed.

A fire was out of the question, so there would be no boiled coffee or cooked meat. They reached into their haversacks and made a supper of hardtack and uncooked salt pork, washing it down with water from their canteens.

The morning dawned with rain still falling. The march began. Men moved through the glue-like mud with difficulty. Mud was a soldier's worst enemy, Jesse decided.

The next morning, December 28, when the bugle's sound aroused him, Jesse emerged from the tent to see that the lower edge of the eastern sky was a strip of orange. It was going to be a sunny day. It will surely be nice not to have to march in rain, Jesse thought happily. But to the delight of just about everyone in the army, it was later announced that there would be no march at all. It was to be a day of rest. No one knew exactly why Rosecrans had decided this, but most everyone was happy about it.

By the night of December 30, the army had reached its goal, the town of Murfreesboro. The soldiers went into position in a roughly straight line some distance behind the west bank of the narrow Stones River. Jesse's brigade was in the middle of the line. Everyone was aware that the Confederate Army was somewhere in front of them, with the little town of Murfreesboro across the river behind it.

chapter six

Battle Losses

The night passed and dawn filled the sky on the last day of the year. There was a thick, chilly mist over everything. Men began to build fires, and with yawns and stretches, started to boil coffee and fry bacon.

Suddenly, the quiet air was ripped with explosions—the eruption of musket fire. Cannons began to boom. In moments, bugles were blaring throughout the camp, calling the regiments to arms. Jesse seized his musket and rushed to fall into place with his company. The sound of musket and cannon fire was rising to a deafening roar. Something about the nature of the landscape was causing the noise of the battle to be magnified, and Jesse knew he would never forget the incredible clamor of this battle.

"I think it's over on the right," Harlow, standing beside him in line, yelled into his ear. Jesse nodded.

The 19th Regiment had gone into the formation known as "line of battle." This was two lines, one behind the other, with enough space between men in the front row for those behind to shoot through. At a command from their regimental commander, Jesse and the others loaded their muskets. Jesse tried to be careful to do everything he had been taught and had practiced at camp. *Take cartridge out of cartridge box. Bite bullet out of cartridge. Pour powder out of cartridge into muzzle. Spit bullet into hand. Push bullet into muzzle. Slide ramrod out of socket. Ram the bullet down. PUT THE RAMROD BACK INTO ITS SOCKET! Cock the hammer. Take out a cap and put it in place.* When he had finished the last move, Jesse took a deep breath of satisfaction.

Now, the order was given to "shoulder arms." Jesse made the four moves that lifted his musket and placed it resting on his right shoulder. The next order was "Left — FACE." Then came "Forward—MARCH." He stepped forward with his left foot as did all the others, and felt himself moving forward. Behind him, the regimental drums began to set the marching pace. Tuh-tuh TAT, tuh-tuh TAT, tuh-tuh TAT tuh TAT TAT.

Jesse found that he felt rather dazed, much as if he were drifting into a dream. He was faintly aware of a scattered banging of muskets going off up ahead of him somewhere. Pickets of each side exchanging shots, he realized dreamily. He moved on, keeping pace with the other soldiers.

The march went on for many minutes, although Jesse had no sense of time. Then, suddenly, came the shouted command, "Regiment—HALT!" Jesse's training took over. He put his foot one more step forward, brought the other foot up beside it, and was at halt. He stood in place and waited for the next command.

It came. "Rest—EASY." Some of the men around Jesse crouched down or knelt to try to make themselves harder targets. Jesse sat down with crossed legs. He found he was much more aware now than he had been while marching. However, he suddenly realized that he was probably in serious danger. He felt panic rising up in him. He wanted to get up and run to the rear.

Was he the only one who felt this way? He looked at some of the other men near him. A number of them were clearly afraid; they were visibly shaking. One man appeared to be crying.

There was a steady rattle of musket fire and an occasional boom of a cannon up in front of them somewhere, but Jesse could not see any sign of enemy troops. He began to feel a little better. Time passed, with nothing happening.

Then, suddenly, there was an eruption of noise. The sound of musketry became a steady roar, pierced by frequent cannon booms. The noise seemed to be coming from Jesse's right, and he realized there must be fierce fighting going on at that end of the Union line. The noise continued into mid-afternoon, sometimes increasing, sometimes becoming less, but still the men of the 19th never saw an enemy and never fired their muskets. As evening slowly darkened the sky, the noise gradually faded away.

Jesse thought it had probably been a bad day for the Union Army. However, there was one bright spot for the 19th Regiment. A number of artillery horses had been killed during the day, and for supper the regiment had broiled horse-meat steaks. Jesse was a little appalled at first, when he learned what he was eating, but he soon decided that fresh horse meat was much better than old salt pork.

In the morning, Jesse and the men of his brigade learned what had happened. A huge Confederate force had managed to slip around the right end of the Union line and began hitting Union regiments from the side, one after another, sweeping them away. The right side of the Union line began to bend back. By the end of the day, Rosecrans's army had been forced into a new position, three miles farther back, only now in the shape of a V instead of a straight line.

There was little fighting on the next day, New Year's Day, but on January 2, 1863, the Southerners made another major attack, this time on the left end of the Union line. The men of the 19th Illinois were near the left end, lying flat on the ground not far from Stones River, waiting to pour fire into any enemy troops that might come at them.

They could see that enemy troops were coming at them this very moment. The land stretching back from the opposite riverbank for some five or six hundred yards was flat and open, and it was swarming with brown-and gray-clad figures, moving forward at a trot. "They'll be here in just a few minutes," Jesse murmured to Harlow, who was lying beside him.

Harlow murmured back, "I know it."

Suddenly, from the right side there was a thunderous crash of artillery. Jesse knew there were four batteries there, at least eighteen guns, and they had all begun to fire. The oncoming rebels were completely in the open and in full view, and shells were bursting among them in a torrent of explosions. It could be seen that they were taking terrible casualties. They were slowing down and spreading out. Many of them were turning back.

An officer on horseback suddenly appeared, riding along the front of the Union line. Jesse recognized him as General Negley, the division commander. "Who will save the left?" he yelled. Jesse understood that he was asking which regiment or group of regiments was willing to try to fight off the Confederate attack that was threatening to overwhelm the army's left flank. The 19th's commander, Colonel Scott, was standing among his men, and Jesse clearly heard him shout back, "The Nineteenth Illinois!" Then he gave the command. "Fix bayonets!" He was calling for a bayonet charge.

The men of the regiment sprang to their feet. Knowing they were going to make a charge, they removed their knapsacks and haversacks and placed them on the ground. You could not fight well during a charge encumbered by equipment. Jesse slid the eighteen-inch-long bayonet out of the scabbard on his hip and slid it onto his musket's muzzle. *Can I stab a man if I have to?* he wondered as he waited for Colonel Scott's next command.

Colonel Scott drew his saber and waved it in the air. "Follow me!" he yelled.

In moments, led by their colonel, the Chicago Zouaves were dashing down to the riverbank in a loose line, with bayonets projecting out in front of them. Most of the men, Jesse included, were yelling at the top of their lungs, a steady wordless shout. Jesse rushed into the river, water splashing around his ankles and swirling around his knees as he advanced, pushing up to his waist as he continued forward. He glanced back and saw that the river behind him was black with the men of another regiment of the brigade, swarming behind the Zouaves. He thought it must be the 18th Ohio. He could hear bullets buzzing past him like angry insects, and saw men going down in the water around him, but he made it to the muddy riverbank and dashed to the top, his bayonet thrust out ahead of him. He was wildly excited.

In front of him, no more than fifty yards away, a double line of men in brown and gray uniforms and a mixture of ordinary clothing was moving toward the river. A Confederate regiment! He could clearly see their faces, and he realized that they were shocked and startled by the sight of the avalanche of blue-clad men pouring over the riverbank at them. Many of them stopped dead, staring with their mouths open. A number turned and ran. Others fired their muskets.

Jesse admired the tremendous courage of these men. They had seen many of their comrades blown to bloody fragments by the artillery fire they had just gone through, and now they had a wall of sharp cold steel rushing at them. It was too much. Suddenly, the whole Confederate regiment was running, and Jesse gave a yell of triumph and heard a tumult of yelling all around him. At a trot, the elated Zouaves chased after the retreating rebels. They could see that another Confederate regiment was coming up behind the one that was fleeing, and as the two units ran into each other they turned into a swirling tangle of confused and frightened men, and then both regiments fled together.

Jesse gave another exuberant yell. The Confederate attack was being turned back. The 19th *had* saved the left!

But the charge was not over. Colonel Scott was nowhere in sight, but the officer who was second in command of the regiment was up in front, waving his sword and leading the 19th on, with the 18th Ohio close behind. They were still under fire from some Confederate regiments ahead, but as they continued to move forward, those regiments began to pull back as the other rebel units had. Jesse realized that the 19th Illinois and 18th Ohio were no longer by themselves; the area around them was full of blue-clad Union troops moving forward. It looked to Jesse as if the Union might have won a tremendous victory.

He found that he was nearly winded and let himself stop and drop to his knees to catch his breath. Most of the men around him were doing the same.

He looked around for Harlow, who had been right beside him when the charge across the river began. He peered about, but although he saw a number of men of the regiment that he knew, there was no sign of Harlow. He cupped his hand next to his mouth and shouted, "Harlow!

Harlow Basset! You around here anywhere?" He waited a moment, listening, but there was no reply. He asked some of the men near him if they had seen Harlow. None had.

A feeling of concern crept over him. He realized that Harlow could have been hit at anytime since the charge began. He could be lying wounded anywhere. Jesse decided he had to go back over every inch of the way the regiment had come after it left the river. The regiment would obviously be resting here for some time, so it would not matter if he were gone for a while.

Getting to his feet, he turned and began to walk back toward the river. He walked very slowly and looked about very carefully. The trouble was there were Union soldiers lying on the ground within sight all along the way, and he went to each one he saw. Some were dead, and he was stunned and sickened at the sight of so many lifeless, contorted, mangled bodies. Jesse had never seen any dead people except those laid out for burial, and he had not known that men could die in horrible positions, with their arms extended upward as if they were reaching for something. He had always thought that people died with their eyes closed, as if they had gone to sleep, and he was deeply disturbed by the wide open glaring eyes in the dead faces. He had not dreamed that human flesh could be so horribly ripped and shredded. He had wanted to see

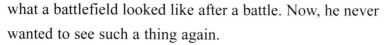

what a battlefield looked like after a battle. Now, he never wanted to see such a thing again.

He had to continue his search, however. Most men he encountered were wounded—some silent, some moaning, some pleading for help. One man was simply calling for his mother. Jesse did what he could to help them, when that was possible. Some were obviously dying and were beyond help. One man asked Jesse if his wound appeared to be fatal. Jesse felt sure it was, but he told the man no.

Every time he came to an outcropping of rock or a swelling of ground that Harlow might have crawled behind if he were wounded, Jesse went to investigate it. Only in one such hiding place did he find anyone: a soldier of the 18th Ohio, shot in leg, who begged him for a drink of water. Jesse unslung his canteen and gave it to the man who drank deeply and thanked him. "Are ye looking for somebody?" he asked, returning Jesse's canteen.

"My best friend," Jesse told him.

"I surely hope ye find him!" the man said earnestly. Jesse thanked him, assured him that the stretcher-bearers would be along soon, and went on his way.

He did not even want to think about the possibility that Harlow might be dead. The fact that he had not found Harlow's dead body was encouraging, and he could think of reasons why he had not found Harlow lying wounded.

Harlow could have been only lightly wounded, which would have entitled him to have dropped out of the charge and make his way back across the river to a field hospital.

However, eventually Jesse came to the riverbank and was immediately struck with a horrifying thought. At one point in crossing the river they had been in water up to their waists—up to the chests of the smaller men. If Harlow had been hit by a bullet then, he could have gone down in water over his head and drowned. His body could be lying on the river bottom now. Jesse found himself standing there, staring down at the slow-moving water. Could Harlow be in *there*?

Jesse decided he could only hope that Harlow had become one of the "walking wounded" and had been able to make his way to a field hospital. Jesse determined to visit every field hospital in the area and look for him. It was turning dusk now, and Jesse was terribly tired, so he would start his search in the morning. After the battle today, the army would not be going anywhere tomorrow.

There would be graves to dig, equipment and ammunition to gather up, Confederate soldiers in hiding to search for, and a host of other details to take care of. Jesse would be able to slip away right after roll call to start his search.

He went back to where the regiment was. In time, it was formed up in a column and trudged back the way it had come on the charge. It splashed through the river, the men pausing to pick up their knapsacks and haversacks lying in line, and plodded on to the tents. Most men were too tired to even think about making a supper and just went to sleep.

Jesse went into his tent and flung himself down. However, tired though he was, he found it difficult to fall asleep. He kept waiting for Harlow to come crawling in. He did not go to sleep for a long time.

chapter seven

A Nation
Changed by War

B y the next day it was known throughout the Union camp that the Confederate Army had withdrawn, leaving behind cannons, equipment, supplies, and a great many dead and wounded men. Jesse had been right in thinking that the Union had won a tremendous victory.

As soon as roll call was over, Jesse left before the first sergeant could come along and sweep him into a work detail. Moving through the company streets, he asked men he met if they knew where the nearest field hospital was, and soon found his way to one. It was a large tent with a strip of red flannel hanging on a post in front of it to indicate that it was a hospital. He sidled through the flap and looked around. There was a sickening smell. For a moment he thought he was going to throw up, but he managed to control himself.

He was horrified by what he saw. Every cot was occupied by a mangled man. He saw men with arms and legs in shreds or totally missing. Less seriously wounded men were lying on the floor—which was actually frozen ground—or propped against the sides of the tent. It was obvious that many of these men were dying. Some might already be dead and just had not been noticed yet.

After checking the men on the cots as best he could, Jesse left the tent. There was a row of corpses lying beside the tent, ready to be taken for burial. Jesse went to carefully look at each one, but none was Harlow.

There were a number of other red-flannel marked tents clustered near this one, and Jesse went into each. He did not find Harlow in any.

Finally, Jesse realized that he was probably never going to find Harlow. Harlow might have been moved to a hospital farther away from these. He might have been wounded, found by stretcher-bearers, and brought to a hospital where he died and was already buried. He might have been shot dead and fallen some place where his body was hidden. He might be at the bottom of the river, as Jesse had already considered.

Jesse gave a long shuddering sigh. His eyes filled with tears. "Sorry, Harlow," he whispered, and gave up looking.

When he got back to his regiment, he told the men of his section of his fears about Harlow. They were shocked and sobered. Jesse learned from them that Colonel Scott, their commander, had been seriously wounded during the bayonet charge and was no longer with the regiment.

"I hope he gets well and comes back," Jesse said earnestly. "He is a brave man!"

Jesse knew that sometimes friends of a man who had been killed in battle wrote letters to the man's wife or family to let them know what had happened. The army did not notify a man's family directly in any way, it merely made a list of the men who had been killed and wounded, and gave the list to newspapers to publish. Often, a wife or family only learned of a man's death or injury by reading his name in a newspaper, long after a battle had taken place.

Jesse decided that he had to write a letter to Harlow's parents telling them of what had happened, otherwise they would almost certainly never know. He hated having to do it, but no one else could, or would. He wrote:

January 3, 1863

Dear Mr. and Mrs. Basset,

I regret to tell you that your son Harlow has been missing since the battle at Stones River on

January 2. I fear that he may have been killed. I searched for him a long time but found no trace. Harlow was a good person, and if he was killed, I am sure that he is now in Heaven.

Your Friend,

Jesse

Jesse hoped his last comment might give Harlow's parents some comfort.

After a few days, the Army of the Cumberland set up a permanent camp around the town of Murfreesboro. It looked as if they might be there a long time. As soon as he could, Jesse wrote a letter to his parents, mainly to give them his new address, so they could write to him. He also told them a little about the battle he had been in. "A battle is a terrible thing," he wrote. "It is terrible to see what men killed by bullets and cannonballs look like." He told them about Harlow. "I fear he is dead. I hope he did not suffer."

When they had some free time, Jesse and several other men of C Company went into Murfreesboro out of curiosity, but quickly became uncomfortable. It was obvious that most of the citizens of Murfreesboro hated Yankee soldiers on sight. The young men were walking down what seemed to be the main street of the town when they noticed that two young ladies were watching them from the other side of the street. When the girls saw the soldiers looking at them, they began to shout "Jeff! Jeff!" Jesse was startled because he thought for a moment they were calling "Jess," and wondered how they could possibly know his name. Then he realized they were calling out the nickname of Jefferson Davis, the president of the Confederacy, to taunt the Union soldiers. To taunt them back, he shouted, "Abe! Abe!" the nickname of the president of the United States. The girls joined hands and ran in the opposite direction.

"You could never get one of these secesh girls to keep company with you," lamented one of Jesse's companions.

"I was keeping company with one in Huntsville," Jesse boasted, but then added, "Sort of."

One day at camp when mail call was held, Jesse received a copy of the January 6 edition of *The Chicago Tribune* newspaper his mother had sent him. The entire front page was devoted to news of the battle he had just been through, which was being called both the Battle of Stones River and the Battle of Murfreesboro.

Reading one of the articles, Jesse learned that the 19th Illinois had lost 124 killed, wounded, and missing out of its total of 340 men. Those were heavy casualties, more than one third of the regiment. They'll need to send us a lot of recruits, thought Jesse. He looked for the list of casualty names, but apparently the army had not given it to the papers to publish yet. Reading on, he was suddenly delighted to see that the newspaper referred to the 19th as "the bravest of the brave." *That's my regiment*, he

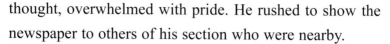

Jesse Bowman

thought, overwhelmed with pride. He rushed to show the newspaper to others of his section who were nearby.

The weeks sped by all too swiftly. Jesse knew that a day would come when there would be a sudden announcement that the army must get ready to march. Then he would be off again, trudging toward some unknown place where a battle might erupt.

The day came. On June 20, the army was told that it would begin a march southward into Tennessee the next morning.

The captain of the company Jesse was in called his men together and explained what was happening. A siege of a Mississippi town called Vicksburg was taking place, but there was danger that the Confederate Army in Tennessee would try to send help to the besieged Confederate force in Vicksburg. General Rosecrans had been ordered by the army commander in Washington to invade Tennessee and block any movement the Army of Tennessee might make toward Mississippi.

The captain went on to explain that to get to the part of Tennessee where the Confederate Army was known to be, the Army of the Cumberland would have to seize a number of passes through some mountains. "What General Rosecrans is going to do is split the army into five parts and send each part up a road that goes to one of the passes," the captain told them. "Our part of the army is General Thomas's whole Fourteenth Corps and the pass we want to capture is called Stevens Gap. We need to get there as fast as we can, so we'll be doing a lot of hard marching!"

In the morning, once again Jesse found himself being issued eighty rounds of ammunition and eight days worth of field rations, and forming up in a column of threes—rows of three men, one behind another. With his musket on his shoulder he stood and waited for the command that would start him marching. He had learned that the brigade he was in had lost a regiment, the 69th Ohio, which had been transferred to another brigade. However, his brigade had gained an artillery battery—Battery M of the First Ohio Light Artillery Regiment, with six cannons.

There was yet another loss and another change. The 19th Regiment had been told that its former colonel, Joseph R. Scott, had died from the wound he received at Stones River, and the 19th was now commanded by Lieutenant Colonel Alexander Raffen.

Jesse had also personally had some changes in his situation. The loss of his tent mate, Harlow, was a problem, because it took two men with shelter halves to create a pup tent. However, Cyrus Bolton had also lost his tent mate, who was wounded at Stones River. The captain solved things by assigning Jesse and Cyrus to be tent mates. Cyrus now filled the right side of the file, the row of three men in which Jesse marched, where Harlow had been. Elisha Graham was still on Jesse's left.

The command to march finally came. Jesse stepped forward, looking about as he did so. Once again, it appeared to him that everyone seemed happy. After a time, he noticed that he was marching past objects lying along the roadside—frying pans, pots, and so on. He smiled, realizing that men had started throwing things away, as they had at the beginning of other marches. I guess all marches must be pretty much the same, he thought. He had heard that some of the other brigades had received a number of recruits recently, and he was willing to wager that it was them doing most of the throwing away. Recruits always tended to load themselves down with things they thought they would need on a march, until they discovered how hard it was to march with a lot of extra weight.

In the early morning darkness two days after the march had begun, it started to rain—a downpour. "We might have known it would begin to rain once Old Rosy started marchin'," growled Cyrus Bolton, marching beside Jesse, who grinned and nodded.

Despite the rain, the various parts of the army were still making good time to reach their objectives. The first pass to be captured, called Hoover's Gap, was reached at nine o'clock that morning. The Confederate force defending the gap was behind a low wall of piled rocks, and there was heavy fighting, but by two o'clock in the afternoon, the pass was in Union hands and the Confederates were retreating. The XIV Corps captured its objective, Stevens Gap, by nightfall, but Jesse's regiment was too far back in the marching column to get into the fighting that took place there.

All the gaps were taken, and the next morning the Army of the Cumberland was approaching the encampment of General Bragg's Confederate Army of Tennessee, which was outside a town called Tullahoma. As soon as Bragg became aware of this, he pulled his army out of Tullahoma.

By July 2, Jesse's brigade had reached Tullahoma and was encamped outside it. A railroad track ran through the town and there were telegraph poles running alongside the track, as there were along most tracks. There was a railroad station in the town and a telegraph office in the station, so Tullahoma could receive news from other places over the telegraph, and today the town was full of news. The people of Tullahoma did not like having Union soldiers in their town of course, but they were willing to talk with them about the news because it was bad news for the Union, and they wanted to rub it in. The news was that a Confederate army had invaded the Northern state of Pennsylvania, and a terrible battle had been raging for two days near a little Pennsylvania town called Gettysburg.

"A rebel army in Pennsylvania! That's terrible!" Jesse said when he heard of this. He shook his head. "That poor little town." He could not help but think of what he had seen in the Alabama town of Athens. He was certain that rebel soldiers would treat a Northern town just like Union soldiers had treated that Southern town. "There's a Pennsylvania regiment in the third brigade; I bet those fellows are worried!"

"It's bad news," Elisha Graham agreed. "If the rebel army wins the battle, and a Union army is beaten on Northern soil, all the copperheads in the North will be raising Cain to make President Lincoln come to terms with the Confederacy." He shook his head. "Copperheads! They're cowardly sneaks, Jesse!"

Elisha knew a lot more about politics than Jesse did, but Jesse understood him. There were people in the North known as copperheads, named after an American poisonous snake, who were against President Lincoln's policies and believed the war was all his fault. There were copperheads in Illinois, Jesse had heard, who had actually wanted Illinois to secede and become part of the Confederacy. Jesse was inclined to agree with Elisha's unkind opinion of copperheads.

Two days later, the news was considerably better. The Confederate Army in Pennsylvania had lost the Battle of Gettysburg and was retreating back into the South. Meanwhile, in Mississippi, the city of Vicksburg had surrendered to General Grant's Union Army. These were two enormous victories for the Union.

"The officers are all celebrating," Elisha told Jesse. "They're in the Colonel's quarters, doing a lot of drinking." He clicked his tongue and shook his head. Being a preacher's son, Elisha did not believe in the use of alcoholic beverages. "But anyway, Captain Grimshaw's orderly told me the colonel said that this would make the war end a lot sooner."

"I surely hope so," Jesse said. He had found that he was no longer enthusiastic about being in a war, as he had been over a year ago when he had enlisted. Seeing so many dead and wounded men and losing his best friend had made him begin wishing he was out of the army. However, he vowed he would keep doing his duty as long as he had to.

In mid-August, General Rosecrans started the army moving again. Day after day, Jesse tramped along with his musket on his shoulder. The bands of different regiments often tried to liven up the march by playing various tunes. There was no rainfall troubling this march; the Tennessee sun burned steadily, hot and hard.

85

As the march moved deeper southward, Jesse was distressed by the views of slavery he was now seeing that would never have occurred to him before. It was clear that most of the big plantations and mansions of wealthy Southerners had been deserted in the face of the oncoming Union Army, and the slaves had simply been left on their own. In every region the blue-clad Union Army passed through, scores and even hundreds of homeless slaves appeared, standing alongside the road, cheering and calling thanks to the soldiers. Shabbily clad men, women, and children were calling out such things as, "We glad you come!" When they saw the national flag, the stars and stripes, come into sight, they would jump up and down, shouting, "Glory! Glory!"

One time, a young man came to the side of the column about where Jesse was, as if he wanted to march with them. "Hey," Jesse called to him, "where are all of you going?"

The young man flung his arms into the air and smiled. "We goin' to follow you-all!" he shouted back. "We goin' to follow you-all to freedom!"

Jesse saw that the black people of the South understood that the purpose of the Union was to destroy the Confederacy and that this would end slavery for good. He began to think that perhaps fighting to help make that happen had a greater significance than he had ever considered. I am fighting to help these people, he suddenly realized.

It soon became obvious that thousands of runaway slaves and those who had been freed by the Emancipation Proclamation had attached themselves to the army and were following along behind it. In the morning and evening, they tried to make themselves useful, bringing wood and building fires, bringing water for coffee and setting it to boil. Many officers took some of these people on as servants, paying them with food and living quarters. General Rosecrans and the other senior officers of the army had organized hundreds of the male ex-slaves into what was called a labor battalion, and had them doing such things as repairing army wagons, disposing of garbage, and other tasks. They were being paid with food, for themselves and their families, and with United States money, with which they could buy things from army sutlers.

By the beginning of September, the soldiers knew that they were heading for the Tennessee city of Chattanooga, where the Confederate Army was known to be encamped. General Rosecrans now sent the XIV Corps to take a position on one side of Chattanooga, another corps to the other side, and halted the rest of the army. Thus, General Bragg had Union forces in front of his army and on both sides. This put him in serious danger, and on September 9, he pulled his army out of Chattanooga and gathered it around a little town about twenty-five miles away. There, he waited for reinforcements he knew were coming.

Rosecrans knew Bragg was getting reinforcements. He called his army back together. The XIV Corps, outside Chattanooga, was ordered to rejoin the rest of the army, and Jesse found himself on the march once more. On September 18, General Rosecrans put the main part of the army into line near a winding stream called Chickamauga Creek in Georgia, near the Tennessee border, about a dozen miles from Chattanooga. He set the men to digging a line of entrenchments. They were completed in the late afternoon, just about the time XIV Corps and the 19th Regiment arrived.

"Old Rosy must be expecting an attack," Jesse commented when he saw the entrenchments.

"I reckon," said Cyrus Bolton, beside him. Both men had learned long ago that digging trenches was strictly a defensive move. When a general felt sure an enemy force was preparing to attack him, he had his men dig trenches to make the attack more difficult. The men in the trenches were protected from bullets by the wall of earth in front of them, but the men coming at them were generally completely in the open.

The 19th Regiment spread out as part of the XIV Corps's line of battle, forming the left side of the army's position, and made camp. Among his friends, Jesse sensed a feeling that things were moving toward a final battle. He was sure they all felt, as Rosecrans obviously did, and as Jesse himself did, that tomorrow the Confederate Army was going to attack.

chapter eight

The Zouave Rush

On the morning of September 19, the Confederate Army of the Tennessee attacked the left side of the Union line. The 19th Regiment was quickly ordered to fall in. Jesse rushed to get his musket, which was stacked with the muskets of the other two members of his file. The regiment went into line of battle together with the other two regiments of the brigade and the Ohio artillery battery.

However, the hours slowly dragged by and nothing happened where the Second Brigade of Negley's division stood waiting. They could tell things were happening elsewhere. The crack of musket fire overlaid with the frequent boom of cannons, blended into a steady roar that indicated the fire was extremely heavy somewhere off to the left.

"I wonder if we're winning or losing," Elisha Graham muttered.

"One thing's for certain," Jesse said grimly. "From the sound of all that fire, lots of men must be getting killed and hurt!"

"I fear you're purely right," Cyrus Bolton agreed.

The hours crept on. Then, suddenly, late in the afternoon, a mounted officer appeared, galloping furiously straight for the house where Colonel Stanley had his headquarters. "That's a messenger in a big hurry if I ever saw one," Elisha Graham said.

Shortly after, Lieutenant Colonel Raffen, who had been in the house with Stanley, could be seen galloping toward his regiment. The commanders of the Ohio and Michigan regiments were also hurrying toward their troops. The color-bearers of each regiment were sliding the flags out of their cases, expecting their units were finally going somewhere. The artillerymen were rushing to bring up the horses that pulled their guns.

Raffen stopped his horse about ten yards from the center of the line and barked out a string of commands. "Regiment—ATTENTION! Left—FACE! Forward—MARCH!" The other commanders were doing the same. The brigade was formed into a column of regiments, with the 19th at the front, marching toward the left end of the Union line of battle.

The farther they marched, the louder the noise of battle became. Jesse had heard all the sounds of battle several times now and could recognize them. A musket bullet, which was a one-ounce piece of lead with a rounded front and flat back, made a buzzing noise like a big insect as it went past. A twelve-pound cannonball of solid iron made a whirring noise. The projectile, called a shell, which was filled with explosive powder, made a hideous shriek that most soldiers believed was the most horrid sound in warfare. When the powder exploded, it broke the shell into many small, sharp-edged fragments. Shell fragments spinning through the air made a whirring sound, moving among trees they made a tick-tick-tick as they struck leaves. Both of these were sounds that made a soldier want to curl himself into a ball and hug the ground. The sound made by a canister, which was a tin can filled with bullets, was a wailing moan as the can was blown apart and the bullets moved through the air in a deadly swarm. Grapeshot, which was clusters of nine iron balls about three times the size of a bullet fired all together, made a moaning sound.

These noises, plus the bangs and booms of muskets and cannons being fired, were what was causing the roar of battle into which the 19th Regiment was marching.

Colonel Stanley halted the brigade in a wooded area, and put it in line of battle to the left of another Union force that was in line. Jesse could not tell if it was a regiment or the remains of a brigade. That it had recently been in action was obvious. There was a row of men with various kinds of wounds lying behind it and a cluster of obviously dead men off to one side. Two doctors were working on a man lying on a bloody wooden table. Most of the wounded men were silent, but several were moaning in pain.

Suddenly, Jesse heard exclamations from some of the men around him, and looked to the front. Confederate soldiers were pouring out of the woods. They were not running, but they were moving quickly. They wore a mixture of clothing: A few had full uniforms of the tan color called butternut, many wore sky-blue pants that had clearly once been part of a Union soldier's uniform, most wore civilian clothing. At the sight of the line of Union soldiers facing them, the Confederates began the high-pitched screeching known as the "Rebel Yell," and began to move forward more quickly. A few of them fired their muskets, even though the range was a little too far for anything but a very lucky hit for a musket ball.

It was not too far for a cannon, however. The brigade's battery, which was loaded and waiting, had a clear field of fire. At a single command, all six guns fired together, with a shattering crash that seemed to make the ground shiver, followed by the moaning sound made by grapeshot speeding through air. Jesse saw the front of the swarming Confederates turn into masses of bloody rags,

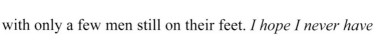

with only a few men still on their feet. *I hope I never have to stand up to anything like that*, Jesse thought.

Despite the horrible slaughter, Confederate soldiers were still coming out of the woods and moving straight toward the Union line.

"Fire at will," called Lieutenant Colonel Raffen. This meant Jesse and the other soldiers could shoot as fast as they were able to. Jesse lifted his musket to his shoulder, remembered to aim low, and pulled the trigger. He did not try to pick out any particular man to shoot at because, although he hoped his bullet would hit someone, he did not want to see it happen. If he killed someone, he did not want to know. Many other soldiers felt as he did, but there were also many who would be delighted to know they had killed a secesher. There were soldiers called sharpshooters, whose purpose was to shoot at any enemy soldier in range, whether a battle was going on or not.

Jesse found himself loading and firing steadily, describing aloud each step in the process, as he had done at Stones River. He knew he was expected to fire at least two rounds a minute, and he was doing his best to accomplish that.

Suddenly, there was another shattering crash from the artillery, and again Jesse saw the front of the Confederate force come apart. It was simply too much for them. They were being fired on by all three regiments of Stanley's brigade, plus the unknown Union force on the right, plus the deadly fire of the artillery battery at almost point-blank range. Jesse knew exactly how they felt. The excitement of a charge suddenly turned into a terrified realization of the danger a soldier was in—he simply wanted to get away from it! Men were turning to rush back into the safety of the woods, and those unable to rush were hobbling. Some were crawling. The field in front of the woods was littered with lying and crouching figures and even clusters of contorted men piled atop one another. The horrible sounds that followed every battle were beginning. Men were moaning, sobbing, screaming, calling for their mothers.

There were also some dead and wounded men in the ranks of the Union regiments, for some of the Confederates had gotten close enough to take some effective shots. When troops went into a line of battle expecting a fight, hospital areas were picked out several hundred yards behind where the battle was expected to be fought, and members of the division Ambulance Corps were sent there with stretchers and ambulances. They would wait there until the battle was over, and then go to look for wounded men and bring them back to a field hospital.

Jesse noticed some ambulances—big-wheeled, horse-drawn, wooden wagons—making their way to where his brigade was in position and looked around to see if any of his friends had been hit. He saw one man he knew—none other than Dickinson—sitting on the ground, clutching a shoulder that was bright with blood. *Well,* thought Jesse, *despite what happened between us, I hope he recovers.*

A fog of white smoke hung over the battlefield as if the air had been painted white, making it very difficult to see anything much over a distance of fifty yards or so. However, Jesse thought he saw movement. So did others.

"They're comin' again!" someone yelled.

Indeed, the Confederates were coming again, bursting from the woods and filling the air with their screeching. *These Southern boys surely do have gumption,* Jesse thought admiringly, raising his musket to his shoulder. "Fire at will," called Lieutenant Colonel Raffen. Jesse fired and began to reload.

The result of this attack was exactly the same as the first one. The Confederates caused a few casualties along the Union line, but their own casualties from the steady blaze of musket fire and crash of cannons finally forced them to pull back into the woods again.

"I wonder if they'll try again?" murmured Elisha. "Those are mighty brave men."

"I doubt it," said Jesse, after a moment. "It's starting to get dark."

They waited, while darkness closed in and twilight became night. There was no longer much, if any, danger of another attack.

Then the lieutenant colonel's voice came from behind them. "Nineteenth Regiment, fall in." There was a loud rustle of some three hundred men climbing to their feet. "About—FACE." Another rustle of men performing the drill movement that turned them around. "Forward—MARCH."

Raffen led them some five hundred feet behind the battlefield. Then came the commands, "Regiment—HALT. Dismissed."

There could be no cooking fires because they could be targets for artillery fire or for a night attack. Jesse reached into his haversack and pulled out two pieces of hardtack and a chunk of raw salt pork. "Elisha? Cyrus? You fellows around here?" he called. The three men located one another and reclined on the ground. They ate their suppers, talked a bit, then lay down on the ground where they were to spend the night fitfully dozing, with their muskets ready in case of a night attack.

The night was cold and it was not easy to sleep. General Rosecrans had ordered a number of divisions into new positions and the sound of their marching disturbed Jesse and the others' sleep. Jesse was also worried about tomorrow. He had enough experience by now to know that today was only the beginning of what would probably be a long and terrible battle.

At about seven o'clock the next morning, Bragg's army attacked again. Jesse was jerked out of sleep by the shrieking of bugles, and he scrambled to his feet clutching his musket. He heard the first sergeant shouting, "C Company, fall in here! C Company, fall in," and ran in that direction. Men were coming from all sides and the regiment was coming together. The other regiments of the brigade were also forming. They were forming in column of march, facing to the left, as ordered by the company first sergeants. The sound of distant musketry and cannons was coming faintly from that direction.

"Anyone know where we're going?" Jesse asked.

"We're probably going to relieve somebody or reinforce somebody," Elisha suggested.

Soon, they were marching. All through the march Jesse felt nervous and excited because he felt sure they would soon be going into action. It seemed to him that they had marched about two miles when the column was halted and faced to the right. Before it was a broad field beyond which was the edge of a forested area. The field was overgrown with high grass and weeds. A company was picked out of each regiment, and the companies were formed into a long line and sent forward into the woods as skirmishers to watch for Confederate troops and give warning of their coming.

Lieutenant Colonel Raffen rode up to the middle of the 19th's line. "Listen, men," he shouted. "If we are attacked, I intend to counterattack! We'll counterattack with the Zouave Rush! This ground is perfect for it."

The regiment began to cheer heartily. They were in favor of using the Zouave Rush. If they had to attack or counterattack, they believed that was the best way.

In preparation for the charge they were going to make, the men began shrugging out of their knapsacks and haversacks. Glancing at the position of the sun, Jesse judged the time to be about ten o'clock. Suddenly, he became aware of motion. A number of blue-clad figures were emerging from the woods, running. They were the skirmishers, and the fact they were running seemed to Jesse to indicate there might be Confederate troops close behind them.

"They're a-comin', boys!" yelled one of the men as they neared the regiment, confirming Jesse's suspicion. The skirmishers broke into groups that headed back to their regiments and got into position.

Lieutenant Colonel Raffen cantered along the front of the 19th Regiment. "Stand fast, soldiers," he ordered.

Moments later, men began to come swarming out of the woods. They seemed to be heading straight for

Stanley's brigade and again the brigade heard the screeching Rebel Yell. They were typical tattered Southern soldiers, most of them without uniforms, like the ones Jesse had seen yesterday. However, among them, on a black-maned reddish-brown horse was a man in a full gray uniform with a row of gold buttons on the coat and gold markings on his shoulders. Jesse thought he might be a general.

"Stand fast!" Raffen ordered.

Jesse grated his teeth and waited. The yelling Confederates were getting closer. What was Raffen waiting for?

Then, Raffen's sword came flashing out of its scabbard. "Forward, double-quick," he roared. "Zouave Rush!"

Jesse hesitated a split second. There was that momentary surge of panic at throwing himself into all-out danger. *You've got to do it*, he told himself, and flung himself forward at a run, with his bayonet extended. At that moment the six cannons of the Ohio light artillery battery at the left of the line all fired together with a tremendous crash. When Jesse had gone about fifteen yards, he dropped to his knees, put his musket to his shoulder and fired, aiming low. Then he fell full length to the ground, rolled over onto his back, and began to reload, reaching into his cartridge box for another round.

When he had reloaded and carefully put the ramrod back where it belonged, he scrambled to his feet and charged forward again for a short distance. He could see that the Confederate forces had stopped moving, and there seemed to be a lot of gaps in it. There were a lot of Confederates on the ground, behind and among those still standing.

Again, Jesse dropped to his knees, lifted his musket, fired, dropped flat, rolled over, and began to reload. Finishing, he sprang to his feet. Instantly, he saw that the situation had changed considerably. Many of the Southerners were running back into the woods, spreading out as they went. Others were standing with their hands in the air. In among the Southerners were many Zouaves with leveled bayonets. There were also soldiers of the brigade's other regiments that must have joined the charge after the Zouaves began their rush.

The Southerner in the gray uniform with gold buttons and trimming was sitting stiffly on his horse with his hands at his side, and Captain Guthrie of the 19th's Company K, was standing before him with a pistol pointed at his chest. Obviously, the captain had made the man his prisoner.

By Golly, if he can do it, so can I, Jesse told himself. There was a Confederate soldier a short distance away holding a musket with a bayonet on it, but making no attempt to do anything. There was a bewildered look on the man's face. However, as long as he held a weapon in his hand, he was a threat to any Union soldier. He either had to surrender—or be made unable to fight.

Jesse ran at the man and brandished his bayonet. "You are my prisoner!" he shouted, trying to keep his voice as low pitched and firm sounding as he could.

The Confederate flinched and dropped his musket with a thud. He raised his hands. "All right, Yank, yuh got me. I surrender."

Jesse grinned. He had captured a prisoner! What a thing to be able to write about in his next letter home to Ma and Pa.

Lieutenant Colonel Raffen was riding about, selecting men to act as guards to take the prisoners to the rear. "Great work, Zouaves," he yelled. "I'm proud of you. But it's not over yet. They'll be coming at us again."

chapter nine

Kings of the Hill

The prisoners were marched back to the rear and the 19th re-formed in the field with the other regiments, some two hundred yards or so from the edge of the woods. Once again, Colonel Stanley sent a line of skirmishers into the trees.

About an hour passed, then the skirmishers were abruptly breaking out from among the trees. "They've been reinforced, boys!" Jesse heard one of them yell.

Suddenly, there was a crash of cannon fire and the shriek of descending shells was piercing the air, sliding down from high pitch to low like a descending scale played on a musical instrument. Jesse and the men around him flung themselves flat onto the ground, their faces pressed into the grass and their shoulders hunched around their heads. There was a cluster of loud explosions, then a man's voice was screaming in pain. Any man hit with a shell fragment could be seriously hurt, or even killed. The fragments could slice vicious bloody gashes in a man's arms, legs, or head. They could penetrate a man's body, destroying a vital organ.

The Southern troops were coming out of the woods. "There are a lot more of them than there were either of the first two times," Elisha observed.

"Yes," Jesse agreed. "I reckon it's a full brigade."

"Fall back! Fall back!" Lieutenant Colonel Raffen was yelling. "Keep together. Make for the top of that hill behind us."

His last word was drowned out by another thunder of cannon booms, followed by the shriek of falling shells. Again, the soldiers of the brigade dived at the earth. There was a spatter of shell explosions. No one screamed this time, but from far down the line Jesse heard someone begin swearing, fiercely.

The brigade was still in a line, moving toward the hill in good order. The men were half turned so that they could halt for a moment and fire a shot at the Confederates who were steadily following, some distance behind but well within range. The Confederates were also firing as they moved forward. Thus, there was a steady pop, pop, pop of musket fire.

When the brigade reached the foot of the hill, the soldiers dashed up the hillside as quickly as they could and went into formation as ordered. This put the 19th Illinois on the right, and the 11th Michigan on the left. Three cannons of the Ohio artillery battery were to the right of the 19th; three were to the left of the Michigan regiment. The 18th Ohio Infantry Regiment was behind the center of the front line, in reserve.

There were some small log buildings a short distance beyond the edge of the hill, and the men of the 19th and 11th regiments tore these up to use the logs to make breastworks in front of themselves. These piles of logs would not prevent enemy soldiers from continuing to move forward, but they would force them to stop a moment to hop over the barrier, and in that moment they could be more easily shot or bayoneted.

The sun was now straight overhead. There was, of course, no attempt to have dinner. Everyone in the brigade believed that at any moment a savage battle was going to erupt.

The Confederate force that had been following Stanley's brigade halted. After a moment, the boom of cannons followed by the shriek of oncoming shells warned the Union troops on the hilltop to take cover as best they could. However, the Confederate artillery commander had misjudged the range, and the shells simply buried themselves in the hillside, some distance from the top.

The Confederate infantry below the hill was being rearranged into a new formation that appeared to be three regiments in line, one behind the other. Jesse believed the Southern commander was going to try to storm the hill with this mass of troops.

To the sound of bugles and shouted commands, the formation began quickly trudging forward up the hill. Jesse heard the welcome command to "Fire at will," coming from the Union company commanders all along the line. He fired into the Confederate formation and began to reload. A steady rattle of musket fire was pouring into the Southerners, and men were going down in twos and threes in the close-packed mass.

Glancing to his right, Jesse saw that there was activity among the three guns of the Ohio battery, and the gunners appeared to be pleased about something. The cannons on the right fired together, and an instant later, the cannons on the left. Looking down from above, Jesse could see what happened as six twelve-pound iron balls slammed into the front of the Confederate formation and continued on through. It was like watching a row of dominoes being pushed over. Men went down in bloody mangled heaps one after another. Sometimes a ball would take out two men at a time, if they were close together. The artillerymen were excitedly cheering the effect of their shots, and Jesse got the feeling they were delighted that the Confederates were using a formation that could be badly hurt by cannonballs at close range.

The Confederates' advance stopped. A few men were continuing to move forward, but some were kneeling or crouching, some were staggering about as if dazed, and some had turned and were running to the rear. There was a sudden crash of cannons as the Ohioans fired again into the milling Confederates. Jesse also fired.

Even as he did all the things he had to do to reload, Jesse saw that the Confederates were pulling back. They were not running, but they were moving at a sort of shuffling trot. When they were off the hill, they kept on going, back toward the woods.

Abruptly he realized the captain was standing over him. "How's your ammunition, Bowman?"

Jesse looked into his cartridge box. "Three rounds, sir!" he said in dismay. That would not carry him through another attack, if there was one.

"How about you, Graham?" asked the captain.

"Four rounds, captain."

"Bolton?"

"I got four rounds, too, sir."

"We're running out of ammunition," the captain said. "All right, there's plenty of dead rebels out on that hillside that have probably got near full cartridge boxes. Graham, Bolton, Bowman, McCabe, Johnston: Get out there and

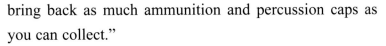
bring back as much ammunition and percussion caps as you can collect."

Jesse put his musket down, darted over the edge of the hilltop, and dashed toward the litter of bodies that lay on the hillside. The first one he came to had no head. That would have horrified him at one time; now it was just one of a number of headless corpses he had seen. He dumped everything out of the man's haversack, then dumped the contents of the man's cartridge case into it along with his percussion cap box.

The next man he came to had a shoulder that had been turned into a mass of tattered flesh and bone fragments by the impact of a cannonball. He had probably bled to death. Jesse dumped this man's cartridges and caps into the haversack and went on. On his way to the next man, he glanced about. There were a number of blue-coated soldiers stooping over prone men on the hillside, so he supposed that soldiers from both the 19th and the 11th Michigan regiments were trying to build up their ammunition supply.

One of the Confederate soldiers Jesse went to was not dead. His foot had been mangled by a cannonball, and although Jesse thought it would almost certainly have to be amputated, he felt the man might survive. "I'll send some of our stretcher-bearers to come carry you to a field hospital," he told the man. The Southerner happily gave him his cartridge box and cap pouch. "Good luck, Yank," he grunted.

When the hillside had been thoroughly searched, the ammunition collectors returned to their companies and turned over their findings. The captain, first sergeant, and sergeants and corporals of Jesse's company worked to determine the amount of ammunition now available and divide it up among those who would be using their muskets in the event of an attack. Jesse was happy to see that he now had twenty-nine rounds. He had reported the wounded Confederate on the hill to his captain, and was gratified to see two stretcher-bearers come pick the man up and carry him back toward their ambulance.

After a while, sounds of battle began to be heard from the right. Some time later, a Confederate force appeared, heading toward the hill. It looked to be about the size of a brigade. "Well, I reckon we're goin' to have to do some more fightin'," Cyrus Bolton said.

The oncoming Confederates were marching confidently to their band's rendition of a favorite Confederate marching song, "The Bonnie Blue Flag." They halted some distance from the bottom of the hill and—Jesse and the other men on the hilltop clearly heard the command—were ordered to "Fix bayonets!" There was a pause, then a single roared "Hurrah!" from hundreds of voices, and they were rushing at the hill, screeching their Rebel Yell. It was a clear message—"We're going to take that hilltop and there is nothing you can do to stop us."

Jesse and all the men of the 19th Regiment fully understood the challenge that the Confederate force was making. It was one of the regiment's color-bearers who answered it. Jesse watched him step forward to the very edge of the hilltop and jam the flagpole of the United States flag into the earth so that the flag stood upright, with the wind fluttering it. That flag was the first thing any Southern soldier would have to pass to step onto the hilltop, and the Union soldiers were telling the Confederates, "In the name of the United States, we hold this hilltop, and you shall not take it!" Jesse saw that the color-bearer of the 11th Michigan Regiment, to the left of the 19th, had also brought his regiment's flag forward to the edge of the hilltop.

The line of Union soldiers along the hilltop opened fire. Men began to go down, here and there, among the figures surging up the hillside, but the Confederates were pausing to fire back, and Jesse felt sure men were going down on the Union line, too. He could clearly see the faces of the men coming toward him, and nearly every one had lips pulled back to reveal tightly gritted teeth. "They really want this hill, boys!" Jesse shouted.

Another flight of shells came shrieking down onto the Union position. They passed over the heads of the two front regiments and landed somewhere near the Ohio regiment in reserve. As if in reply, the three guns on the left side of the Union front line fired a trio of balls into the Southern troops on the hillside. Jesse saw the trail one of them left, as men were suddenly thrown aside or knocked over as they were hit.

Despite the storm of musket and cannonballs hurtling into them, the Confederates were still moving up the hill. They were also continuing to pour a hail of lead at the hilltop. At least half a dozen times Jesse had heard the buzz of a bullet going past him. Some men did not hear those bullets, Jesse knew. You did not hear the bullet that killed you.

The Confederates continued to press forward through the heavy fire that was being poured into them, bent over as if they were moving through a driving rainstorm. A lot of them were pausing to fire and load, so the Union line was being lashed with vigorous fire, too. Sometimes a Confederate would nearly reach the Union breastwork, when he would fire at point-blank range, then fall back a distance to reload and move forward again.

The troops were now almost face-to-face. Jesse was no longer able to risk trying to reload; he was using his bayonet to defend himself. He stabbed at a man passing in front of him, then used his musket barrel to ward off the blade of a man stabbing at him. This was some of the hardest fighting he had ever done. On both sides, men were viciously stabbing with bayonets and using their muskets as clubs. It was as if they refused to use muskets against their opponents at this stage in the battle; only brute hand-to-hand combat would do.

To his dismay, Jesse saw that the Confederate flag was nearly at the top of the hill. *They're pushing us back,* he realized.

Suddenly, he saw a flag, the stars and stripes, flash past him among a swarm of Union troops. For a split second he saw a face he knew. It was a soldier of the 18th Ohio! The 18th Ohio, which had been standing in reserve until now, had come forward to reinforce the Illinois and Michigan regiments, and help prevent the Confederate brigade from getting onto the hilltop. The Ohio regiment's color-bearer was leading the regiment straight forward against the Confederate flag that was pushing onto the hilltop. For an instant, the two flags were so close together that they seemed to be snapping in the wind at each other. Then, Jesse saw clearly what happened as the Confederate color-bearer received a death wound. With blood welling out of his chest, he staggered back and then, even as he was obviously dying, to keep his flag from being captured he flung it behind him as far as the strength left in him would allow. A Confederate soldier seized it, and began to carry it away—to the rear. Confederate soldiers began to follow it down the hillside. The man who had carried it nearly to the edge of the hill now lay facedown and unmoving, only a few feet from the Union breastwork.

The Confederates were clearly withdrawing. Their fire had fallen away to almost nothing, and with low ammunition and no reason to keep shooting at them, the Union troops stopped firing as well. A sudden silence descended upon the battlefield.

Jesse became aware that twilight was gathering. He was also aware that he had just passed through a long period of having been in probably the greatest danger of his life, and he had survived it.

"Praise be to the Lord," Elisha Graham proclaimed.

"I wonder how many casualties we took," Jesse gasped. "A lot, I bet."

The brigade stayed in position for a good hour after the firing had stopped, and Jesse supposed the commanders wanted to be sure there was no other attack forthcoming. The men in the line sat or reclined. As usual after a battle, the horrible sounds of pain and dying were coming from the hillside.

At about eight o'clock that night, the 19th and other regiments were ordered to fall in. They were marched

down off the other side of the hill, ordered to turn right, and marched some distance until they came to a road. There they were turned to the left and continued marching several hours. The night was silent—there was no sound of cannon or musketry. Jesse wondered where they were going and what had happened. No one knew, except probably the officers, but they did not provide any information.

The moon had set, so it was probably about eleven o'clock when they came to where the road ran through a town. There were no lights on in the town, and it seemed empty. The brigade was ordered to encamp outside the town, but with no tents pitched and no fires allowed for any purpose.

When the men of the 19th had an opportunity to sit together and talk, they did learn some rather upsetting things. Some of the soldiers of the Southern brigade that had made the attempt to capture the hill, which Jesse learned was called Snodgrass Hill, had been captured and questioned. Corporal Martin had been in on the questioning, and he told Jesse and the others what had been found out.

Confederate General Bragg's Army of Tennessee had been reinforced by a small army of two divisions under the famous Confederate General James Longstreet. Early that morning, Longstreet had led his force on an assault against the Union right side and discovered something—there was a wide gap in the middle of the Union right.

Immediately, Longstreet had taken his divisions crashing through the opening into the side of the Union forces on the right. Hit from the side and rear, regiment after Union regiment was swept away. According to the Southern prisoners, the whole Union right side had collapsed, and half of Rosecrans's army was gone, retreating in panic to the city of Chattanooga.

There was silence after Martin delivered his news. Then Elisha Graham asked, "Do you believe it?"

"I believe he told us what he saw and what he believed happened," Martin replied. "He might be wrong about some things, but we know there was a lot of trouble over on the right today. We could hear it!" They could hear his voice shake as he spoke. "I think that all that's left of the army is what's been fighting over here on the left today, under General Thomas. He's kept us together, and he'll get us out o' this!"

Then, Jesse became aware that the regimental master sergeant was softly making his way from group to group. "Fall in, *quietly*," he was telling them, stressing the word "quietly." "Don't anyone leave the ranks for any reason. Make sure no one is left here. Carry them if you have to!"

With the others, Jesse got to his feet and trudged back to the road. At that moment, an artillery battery came past, the guns fastened to their limber chests and harnessed to their horse teams. There was just enough light for Jesse to see that the wheels of the guns and limbers were wrapped with blankets, rugs, and rags to muffle the sound they might make as much as possible. He suddenly realized what was happening.

"Elisha. Cy. We're retreating," he whispered.

Shortly, they were ordered to resume marching. They shuffled along for about an hour, until they were told they could halt and fall out. There, on a broad expanse of land that appeared in the darkness to be a harvested cornfield, Jesse dropped to the ground and his exhausted body was almost instantly captured by sleep.

He was awakened very early the next morning. At about six o'clock, the brigade was ordered to march. After about an hour it reached a hill where it was put in position facing toward the rear. Occasionally, an infantry or artillery unit, or a few mule-drawn supply wagons, would come up the road from the rear, pass the hill, and continue on.

"It looks like General Thomas has made us the Rear Guard," Corporal Martin told Jesse and his friends when he passed by them later in the morning. "That's an honor! It shows he has real confidence in us."

"Think we'll have to fight 'em?" Cyrus Bolton asked.

"I'm surprised we haven't had to fight 'em already," Martin replied, rubbing his chin, thoughtfully. "When an army's retreating, that's the enemy's best chance to wipe it out. I'm surprised there hasn't been rebel cavalry swarming over us all morning! Either Old Rosy managed to outfox General Bragg somehow, or else Bragg has made one big mistake by not chasing us!"

The brigade stayed in position for the rest of the day. The troops moving past became fewer and fewer and from about noontime on, the road stayed empty.

"Well, I guess everybody got away," Elisha commented later in the afternoon.

"We haven't yet!" Cy pointed out. "I won't feel safe until we get to wherever we're supposed to be goin', with rest o' the army around us!"

Jesse nodded vigorously.

A little before midnight, the brigade was again ordered to form up and quietly begin marching. Trudging along, Jesse realized that his brigade must be the very last unit of the Army of the Cumberland to have left the battlefield. That must be an honor of some kind he decided, yawning.

At about 3 A.M. on September 22, the brigade reached the outskirts of the city of Chattanooga. The men were told to fall out where they were. Once again, Jesse fell asleep on the ground, in the middle of an open field, clutching his musket.

chapter ten

Under Siege

Jesse awakened to the sound of voices mingled with a strange sssshuff—sssshuff—sssshuff noise. Opening his eyes, he discovered that the voices were those of many hundreds of men in a line that apparently stretched around the outskirts of Chattanooga, and the "sssshuffing" noises were being caused by the shovels they were using to dig into the earth. There was also an occasional clang as a shovel hit a buried rock. The men were digging trenches. He saw that a number of homes around the outskirts of the city, apparently deserted by their owners, were being turned into forts by having rocks piled around them. He also saw there were several batteries in position, their guns pointing into the distance out beyond where Jesse's regiment had encamped. It seemed clear that the Army of the Cumberland had somehow been able to avoid total defeat at Chickamauga and had managed to seize control of Chattanooga, and General Rosecrans was now fortifying the city against attack. Chattanooga sat inside a curve of the broad Tennessee River, and the fortifications consisted of a three-mile-wide semicircle running from one riverbank to the other. Thus, one side of the city was protected by a river running in front of it, and the other side was protected by a wall of fortifications.

The familiar voice of the C Company first sergeant was calling the command to "Fall in," and Jesse scrambled to his feet, as all the soldiers of the 19th were doing.

With Lieutenant Colonel Raffen and his staff cantering ahead of them on their horses, the men of the 19th marched into Chattanooga behind their colors, toward the part of the city that had been assigned to them for their encampment. They passed through several streets, passed a number of handsome houses, and saw some imposing buildings in the distance.

The regiment was finally halted within a square open area that they learned was called Cameron Hill. It had several streets leading into it, houses on three sides, and a large wooded area, composed mostly of oak trees, on the fourth side. The houses appeared to all be empty. Jesse had noticed that there had been no civilians in sight as the regiment had been marching through the city, and he wondered if perhaps the people of Chattanooga had been made to leave.

Cameron Hill also had an excellent view of some of the land surrounding Chattanooga. For Jesse, who had grown up in the city of Chicago where the land was flat for miles and miles all around, the land around Chattanooga was certainly different. It was bumpy, hilly, and mountainous. On the southeastern side of Chattanooga was a long stretch of high hilly ground called Missionary Ridge. Some distance in front of the ridge was a small bumpy hill known as Orchard Knob. West of Missionary Ridge was a triangle-shaped, thousand-foot-high mountain called Lookout Mountain.

Within a few days of Jesse's arrival in Chattanooga, all this high ground overlooking the city was abruptly occupied by the troops of General Bragg's Confederate Army. On one late September day, as evening turned into night, Jesse was astounded to see thousands of twinkling lights spread across the length of Missionary Ridge, clustered on the top and upper sides of Lookout Mountain, and nestled among the bumps of Orchard Knob. Rebel troops had come onto these positions during the day and now had lit their evening campfires. It looked as if half the stars in heaven had come down to settle around Chattanooga and the Union Army within it.

"The rebels have really got us surrounded," Jesse observed.

"Yup. You're in a siege, Bowman, a genuine siege," Corporal Martin said.

"Well, but—what does that mean, corporal? Are they going to try to attack us in here?"

Martin shook his head. "I don't think old Bragg would *dare* try to attack. Old Rosy's fortifications are too good, and the rebels might lose half their army. No, I think Bragg will just sit tight and try to starve us out."

Jesse stared, puzzled. "How could he do that? We've got a whole city full of food."

"It doesn't matter how much food we've got right now, we'll eat that up in no time," Martin told him. "You have to replace the food you eat, Jesse. You have to get more food from somewhere. I don't know where we're getting our supplies from now, but they're coming from a secret place by a secret way, and if Bragg can find out what that secret way is, all he has to do is block it off with a few thousand men, and we'll start to starve. And after we starve for a while, we'll be ready to surrender. Bragg won't have to take Chattanooga with a big battle—he can starve us out of it. That's one of the main things you have to worry about in a siege, Jesse."

The soldiers of the 19th discovered there was a plentiful supply of trimmed logs lying unused nearby, so one of the first things they did was improve their living conditions. With logs and dirt they constructed huts that could hold from four to six men. These huts were far better than pup tents for providing protection from rain, wind, and chilly air. For some reason Jesse was not aware of, the huts became known as shebangs. "How are things at your shebang?" soldiers would ask one another.

On the morning of September 29, Jesse was shown another method of siege warfare he had not been aware of. There was a loud boom from the direction of Lookout Mountain. Most everyone within sight of the mountain looked toward it and many thought they saw a patch of white smoke hanging over an area near the top of it. In one small corner of Chattanooga, soldiers heard a rustling sound in the sky that grew louder until, abruptly, there was a shattering crash and the wall of an empty house was smashed in as if by an extremely heavy blow.

There were plenty of men in the army who knew what had happened, and the news quickly spread.

"The rebs have put siege guns on Lookout Mountain!"

"The rebs are shootin' at us from Lookout Mountain with siege guns!"

Siege guns were special big cannons that fired a heavy solid iron ball for a long distance. Their sole purpose was to fire into cities and fortresses, causing as much damage and terror as possible. Cause terror they did. For Jesse and many of the other younger soldiers, there was real concern about having to live under a constant rain of huge cannonballs smashing things. But then, the soldiers made a discovery. The siege gun balls were so heavy and slow-moving that it took them a long time to reach their target. It was actually possible for soldiers to watch the flight of a siege cannonball, judge where it was going to come down, and move away from the area.

After only a few days, apparently aware that the bombardment was not having any effect, General Bragg ordered the guns on Lookout Mountain to stop firing. However, shortly after the siege guns stopped being a problem, the Union forces in Chattanooga were shocked by some events that affected them in another way.

On the morning of October 3, the Army of the Cumberland in Chattanooga awakened to see a huge cloud of smoke hanging in the air to the northwest. During the day there were explosions and the sounds of many musket rounds going off. The soldiers gathered in groups, trying to figure out what was going on.

"It sounds like a battle," Elisha Graham commented. "Do you suppose some Union troops have been sent to help us and got into a scrap with the rebs?"

"That's not battle smoke," Jesse pointed out. "Battle smoke's white—you know that, Elisha—and that smoke is black. It looks like wood fire smoke to me."

"Maybe it's a town burnin'," Cyrus Bolton suggested. "Maybe a Union army has found a town full o' reb soldiers and is fightin' a battle and burnin' the town."

No one could think of a better possibility, although they spent much of the rest of the day discussing it.

The next morning there was another mystery. Another mass of smoke hung in the sky, but this was in a different place, some distance from where the first smoke had been. There was no sound of weapons being fired.

"What in tarnation is goin' on?" exclaimed Cy Bolton.

"Well—maybe it all has nothing to do with us," said Jesse, hopefully.

It was several days until the common soldiers learned what had happened. A cavalry unit had been sent out to investigate and discovered that a large Confederate cavalry force had been searching for the route used to bring supplies to the Union forces in Chattanooga—and had discovered it. On the morning of October 3, the Confederates had caught a Union supply train of eight hundred wagons packed with food and ammunition, each drawn by four mules. The wagon train was guarded by twelve hundred Union soldiers, but they were outnumbered four to one by the Confederates and, after a brief battle, surrendered. The Confederates spent the next eight hours burning the wagons and everything in them, and shooting the mules. It was the burning wagons that filled the sky with the smoke seen from Chattanooga, and the burning, exploding ammunition, and shooting of the mules that had made it sound as if a battle was going on. On the next night, the Confederate force located a major Union supply depot and burned it as well.

Jesse Bowman had hoped that the mysterious smoke seen in the sky for two days would not have anything to do with the Union troops in Chattanooga, but it did. The loss of so many supplies had an immediate effect. An announcement was made to the troops that daily rations would have to be cut by one quarter. With the main supply route having been located by a Confederate cavalry force, there was now only one route for supplies to come into Chattanooga—a high narrow mountain road in poor condition that could only be used by very small wagon trains and could not carry much. Jesse remembered what Corporal Martin had told him about the possibility of starving during a siege, and he began to worry a little.

"The government and the War Department ought to be doing something to help us," he complained to his friends.

However, word began to race through Chattanooga that thousands of Union soldiers and dozens of guns, two whole divisions from the Army of the Potomac in the East, had been sent to the city on this railroad to reinforce the Army of the Cumberland. They were encamped around the town of Bridgeport, only a few miles from Chattanooga.

"Why don't they come into town, then?" Cyrus wondered.

"Shucks, Cy, there's not enough food for *us* here, how could two more whole divisions be fed?" Elisha told him.

Rations were coming in, but they were dreadfully few. There were days when men got no more than two or three hardtack crackers to eat. Tales sprang up about how starving soldiers were trying to deal with the lack of food. It was said that some soldiers of a Kansas regiment had discovered a small dog that had wandered into the city from somewhere. They shot it, skinned it, cut it up, and cooked it. Another story was that soldiers were stealing the small amounts of parched corn and dried oats that were being supplied as rations for the army's horses and mules. That this story was true, Jesse knew for sure, for he had been put on duty four hours a day as an extra guard to see that the gaunt, starving animals were not robbed by gaunt, starving soldiers.

As for Jesse's regiment, the 19th Illinois suddenly found that it had been handed a tremendous stroke of luck. The camp area assigned to it when it had arrived contained a great many oak trees, and one of the Illinois boys recalled from his childhood that acorns, the nuts produced by oak trees, could be roasted and eaten. When this

126

information was spread, every soldier of the 19th not on duty hurried to begin foraging beneath the easily recognized trees for fallen acorns. This became a daily activity that Jesse and others eagerly engaged in. Roasted acorns became a very important addition to the 19th's food supply.

On the morning of October 20, another rumor began to race through the Army of the Cumberland. It was said that General Rosecrans had been removed from command. It seemed to be true, because Rosecrans was seen leaving on a train to the east that afternoon.

Things began happening very quickly. On the evening of October 23, General Ulysses S. Grant arrived. He went immediately to the headquarters of General Thomas.

It was obvious that Grant was in charge of everything, and the news soon leaked out that he had been put in command of the entire western theater of war by President Lincoln. He immediately went to look over the Confederate positions surrounding Chattanooga, and his first visit was to Cameron Hill, the encampment of the 19th Illinois, where he could get a good look at Lookout Mountain and Missionary Ridge. He was accompanied by General Thomas, and the Illinois soldiers pressed around the two generals as closely as they dared. With hundreds of others around, Jesse could not get very close, but he did catch a glimpse of the two men.

It soon became obvious that Grant had appointed Thomas as the new commander of the Army of the Cumberland, to replace Rosecrans. Because of his courage and determination at Chickamauga, Thomas had been given the nickname "The Rock of Chickamauga" by the newspapers, and the soldiers had adopted it. They were fond of Rosecrans, but they admired Thomas. The men of Thomas's Corps believed that Thomas had saved the Army of the Cumberland from destruction. "I'm sorry Rosy is gone," Jesse remarked to his friends Elisha and Cyrus, "but I'm glad we got Thomas!"

The last Confederate position Grant looked at was a town called Brown's Ferry. If the Confederate troops could be pushed out of Brown's Ferry, a supply line could be linked up from Chattanooga to Bridgeport, and from Bridgeport to all the vast supply sources in Union territory in the East. Grant gave the order.

Late on the night of October 26, fourteen hundred men of General Hazen's Brigade of Thomas's army got into specially made boats and rowed up a bend of the Tennessee River. They disembarked several miles from Brown's Ferry and attacked.

Everyone in the Army of the Cumberland knew what was happening. Jesse and his friends, as well as most of the soldiers in Chattanooga, were staring out over the river toward the direction of Brown's Ferry, but there was a row of hills between Brown's Ferry and Chattanooga. Nothing could be seen except low flashes in the sky, cannon fire reflecting off low clouds. The noise that could be heard told a tale, however. The booming of cannons and the steady popping of musket fire that ran together until it became a single continuous sound indicated a heavy fire fight. "That's a real scrap goin' on," Cy muttered.

Most of the soldiers finally fell asleep. Jesse found himself dozing and waking. The fact was, he was worried. What would happen if the new supply line could not be established? Would the army have to pull out of Chattanooga and retreat? *Could* it pull out, or would it have to surrender? The thought of possibly having to spend years in a Confederate prison chilled him. Some of the stories told about prison life were horrible.

He fell asleep and was awakened by the sound of bugles blowing First Call. The sky was light. There was no sound. Whatever had happened at Brown's Ferry was over.

There was no news until nearly noon. Then, excitement seemed to come swirling through the city. Men were shouting and cheering. Some of the regimental bands struck up marches or popular tunes. The rebels had been driven out of Brown's Ferry—it was in Union hands. The supply line would be established!

It took several days, but then hardtack and other things began to appear in greater quantities. Rations were increased. Meat became available. The soldiers in Chattanooga began to refer to the new supply line as the "Cracker Line."

It seemed to Jesse and all the other soldiers of the Army of the Cumberland that something big was building up. The reinforcements that had been sent from the east had increased the size of Grant's force, and it was well-known that part of the Union Army of the Tennessee commanded by General William T. Sherman was marching through Tennessee to join Grant at Chattanooga. There was talk that Grant might have as many as fifty or sixty thousand men when they all got together. What does he plan to do with us, Jesse wondered. He did not believe Grant intended to let all of them just sit in Chattanooga in case the rebels attacked it. Jesse felt that Grant was going to go out after the rebels. That was the sort of general he was.

Jesse was surer than ever that something would soon happen when he learned that General Thomas had reorganized the Army of the Cumberland. It seemed to Jesse that whenever an army got reorganized it was soon in battle. General Buell had reorganized the army and it had been in the Battle of Perryville within a short time. General Rosecrans had reorganized the army and headed straight for Murfreesboro and Stones River.

Even with the reorganization, Jesse found that he was still in the XIV Corps, the First Division, and the Second Brigade, but the brigade had changed considerably. The 19th's staunch comrades of the 11th Michigan Regiment, who had been beside them on Snodgrass Hill at Chickamauga, were still with them, but the 18th Ohio was gone. However, they had regained another old friend, the 69th Ohio, which had been with them at Stones River.

The other change in the brigade was a source of much interest. Four new regiments had been added—very special regiments. They were the 15th, 16th, 18th, and 19th regiments of U.S. Infantry. These were what were known as "Regular Army" troops of the United States Army. Soldiers of a brigade were always a little doubtful when new regiments came into the brigade, wondering what sort of fighters they might be, but there were no doubts about these men for Jesse or anyone else in the Second Brigade. They were veterans whose lifetime profession was fighting wars!

The troops of the new brigade began to drill together. On the morning of November 22, the Army of the Cumberland was formed up in the streets of Chattanooga. Soon, Jesse was again marching along with his musket on his shoulder. The siege of Chattanooga was over; the battle for Chattanooga was about to begin.

131

chapter eleven

Among the Wounded

O n November 22, everyone marching in the ranks of the Army of the Cumberland knew they were headed toward the bumpy hill known as Orchard Knob that sat in front of Missionary Ridge. It was crisscrossed by entrenchments filled with Confederate soldiers who would have to be driven off the hill so that Union troops could use it for launching an attack on Missionary Ridge. That night, the Army of the Cumberland made its camp below Orchard Knob.

The attack was launched with bugle calls at 1:30 on the afternoon of the next day. General Thomas had appointed three divisions, about twenty-five thousand troops, to do the job of clearing the Confederates off Orchard Knob. None of the divisions was the division to which the 19th Illinois belonged, so Jesse and his friends watched from below as their comrades moved onto Orchard Knob and began their task.

The Confederates fought hard and courageously, as they always did, but they were outnumbered and simply unable to hold the position. When the troops watching below saw that the only flags to be seen on Orchard Knob were those of Union regiments, a huge cheer went up. The rest of the Army of the Cumberland moved up onto Orchard Knob, so one of the campfires that glowed there that night belonged to Jesse and his friends. It seemed an odd twist of fate to him, that he, who had so often watched the sparkling campfires on Orchard Knob while he was in Chattanooga, should now be sitting at one here himself.

At 8:00 a.m. on the morning of the next day, November 24, the second move of the Union plan was made. The two divisions of the Army of the Potomac, plus one from the Union Army of the Tennessee, began the advance on Lookout Mountain. They were about ten thousand strong and led by a general known as "Fighting Joe" Hooker.

It was a chilly morning, and there was thick gray fog clinging to Lookout Mountain. The division leading the Union attack put its brigades into three lines, one behind the other, with a line of skirmishers in front. In this formation, it began to move toward the mountain through the fog. Because of the fog, Jesse, watching from Orchard

Knob, could not see any of this. But when he heard the sudden scattered popping of musket shots, he knew the Union skirmishers and Confederate pickets had gotten close enough to see each other and opened fire.

The Union division commander moved his troops to the side of the mountain and they began to climb up, over boulders and fallen tree trunks. The Confederate troops waiting on the mountainside saw them coming and tried to defend their position, but they had not been expecting the Union force to come at them from the side, and were driven off by a fierce bayonet charge. The Confederates were heavily outnumbered, and by late afternoon, Lookout Mountain was in Union hands.

November 25 was to be the day of the crowning blow of the Union plan, the taking of Missionary Ridge. Along its base were trenches filled with Confederate soldiers. Along the top were trenches filled with more Confederate troops and cannons. These were strong defenses.

The Army of the Cumberland waited on Orchard Knob to make an advance on the trenches at the foot of Missionary Ridge. Jesse's brigade was lying down in a line of battle in a wooded area, straight in front of the ridge where the Confederate army waited.

The soldiers of the Army of the Cumberland were not at all happy with the part they had been given in this battle. Actually, they were angry and hurt. They felt they were being treated as second-rate troops because they had been defeated at Chickamauga. Instead of taking part in the main attack, on top of Missionary Ridge, they had been ordered to make a secondary attack on the trenches at the bottom of the ridge.

The men of the 19th Illinois were particularly bitter. "*The Chicago Tribune* called us the 'bravest of the brave,'" said Jesse, recalling the newspaper story about the Battle of Stones River, "but I guess we're not brave enough for General Grant!"

"We've got to change his mind, somehow," grumbled Cyrus Bolton.

"I've got an idea," said Elisha. His eyes were glinting. "We've got to show him what we can do. We've got to take things into our own hands. When we get to that trench, instead of stopping like we're ordered to—we keep right on going up the ridge to the top!"

The other two men stared at him with widening eyes. Jesse snapped his fingers. "Right!" he exclaimed. "Pass it along the line." To the left and right along the line of prone men, heads began to come together. An idea began to grow in the ranks of the Army of the Cumberland.

There had been sounds of gunfire from the top of the ridge since after dawn. At times it died away, then it would break out into a steady roar for a long time. From their position, the men of the Army of the

Cumberland could see nothing. Hours passed. Then, at about three o'clock, from behind them came the boom of a single cannon.

The signal for the attack on the trenches was to be six cannon shots, with the army starting to move forward on the last shot. When the single cannon shot sounded, Jesse and many others began to count. "One." A sudden silence fell over the entire army. *It was not the silence of men who were fearful*, thought Jesse, *it was more like a feeling of determination.* Before the second shot even boomed, the regiments were forming up, and before the sixth shot was fired, they were all moving forward.

Emerging from the woods, Jesse found himself on a broad field about a fifth of a mile long. Commands were ringing out—"Forward, Double-Quick—MARCH!" With the others, Jesse increased his pace to the steady jogging trot that was known as "double-quick time." The Confederates in their trenches had opened fire now, a few shots at first, gradually increasing to a rippling roar. The line of skirmishers across the Union front was firing back, as rapidly as they could. Shells, fired from cannons up on the ridge, were shrieking down to burst among the advancing Union troops. Jesse gritted his teeth as he heard the deadly whir of shell fragments slicing through the air around him, but he did not throw himself to the ground. He did not want to stop; he wanted to get to those trenches.

Men had gone down all around him, but no one was turning back, no one was stopping.

The Union force reached the trenches and flowed into them. Some Confederate soldiers began to pull out, turning and scurrying up the hillside. Some threw down their muskets and raised their hands. Some tried to fight and were shot, bayoneted, or clubbed senseless with musket butts.

Jesse reached the edge of the trench and leaped into it. Directly in front of him, a tattered rebel soldier about his own age with a pale, terrified face was standing with hands thrust into the air. Jesse gave his head a backward jerk toward the Union lines. "Go to our lines and turn yourself in," he snarled. The man scrambled to obey.

Now was when the Army of the Cumberland was supposed to stop and let the other two armies do the job of assaulting the ridge and driving the Confederates off it. But the men of Thomas's army were still not stopping. The regiments kept on going. In moments, the bottom of the ridge was swarming with Union soldiers making their way upward as swiftly as they could. It was obvious that the soldiers of the Army of the Cumberland had made their decision about how they would prove their worth to General Grant. No one could doubt that they were beginning a *charge* up Missionary Ridge!

Jesse's regiment was among the first ones charging up the hillside. The Confederate fire from the ridge above was heavy. Jesse saw men going down in front of him and around him. He felt no fear, only a wild excitement.

Even among all the confusion, the noise, the death, the pain, Jesse realized that it was not just Northern soldiers going up the hill. Every regiment in the Army of the Cumberland had a number of runaway slaves with them. They cooked and washed for the soldiers, kept the encampment area clean, gave haircuts and trimmed whiskers, and made themselves useful in a great many ways. Now they were wholeheartedly joining in the fight to drive the Confederate force off Missionary Ridge. Jesse saw that every regiment had a number of black men moving along with it, carrying muskets with fixed bayonets, many wearing blue Union uniform coats. They all wore looks of determination on their faces.

In all the regiments, soldiers were beginning to shout "Chickamauga!" It was a warning to the Confederates on the ridge that the Army of the Cumberland was going to take revenge for its defeat at Chickamauga.

The regiments were taking on a strange shape. Each regiment was being led by the color sergeants who carried the national flag and the state flag. Behind them were the four men who formed what was called the Color Guard that marched behind the flags in regimental parades. Behind them, the regiments had apparently gathered into masses with the boldest men at the front, the others forming a broader mass behind. Thus, each regiment was moving in a loosely triangle-shaped formation, with the flags at the point, the rest of the men fanning out behind them.

The flag bearers at the front were a major target, of course, and Jesse saw Color Sergeant Grimes suddenly go down. A man behind him flung his musket away, darted forward, and snatched up the flag. Lifting it high overhead to catch the breeze, he now led the regiment forward. Jesse and the men around him roared out a cheer.

Men ahead of him were swarming over the top of the ridge. He had nearly reached the top himself when something slammed into his right leg, above the knee. It felt as if someone had swung a musket butt with all his might and smashed it into his leg. Suddenly, the leg gave way beneath him and he pitched to the ground. His leg was pounding with pain, and he saw that a dark red stain was spreading out on his sky-blue pants leg. He realized that he had been shot.

Jesse had only one thought—to get to the top of the ridge with the other men of his regiment and army. He tried to scramble to his feet, but his leg simply would not work. He was unable to stand. He could only lie there and watch longingly, as Union soldiers rushed past him. He

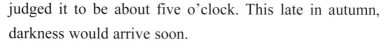

judged it to be about five o'clock. This late in autumn, darkness would arrive soon.

Men continued to rush past him. He watched them leap over the top of the ridge and disappear as they continued down the other side. The sounds of musket fire were moving away, which Jesse felt sure meant that the Confederates were pulling back, withdrawing, retreating. The cannon fire from the top of the ridge had stopped completely, which could only mean that all the enemy cannons there had either been pulled away or captured.

The men going past him became fewer and fewer. Finally, there were no more. There was silence, except for a faint, apparently very distant, whisper of sound that might have been battle noise, very far away. There were also, of course, the sounds of wounded men in pain, lying on the hillside as Jesse was.

It was dark before Jesse was discovered. He saw a steadily glowing light swinging from side to side coming toward him and believed it must be a lantern hanging from an ambulance. "Help," he called weakly. "I can't walk."

The light bobbed closer then stopped. Jesse heard the sound of feet hitting the ground, and saw that a man had detached the lantern, holding it high, and was hurrying toward him. He wore a uniform just like Jesse's, but on his sleeves were the green entwined snakes that were the symbol of the Army Medical Corps, showing that he was the kind of soldier known as a hospital steward. Jesse knew soldiers who did not like hospital stewards, saying they were cowards who were afraid to fight in battles. However, Jesse had heard stories of stewards risking their lives to get wounded men to safety. *There is more than one kind of bravery*, he thought.

The steward bent over Jesse, shining the lantern light on him to see his wound. "What regiment, soldier?"

"Nineteenth Illinois Infantry," Jesse answered in a weak voice.

"That's in our division. We'll have you to a hospital in no time." He was joined by another man bringing a stretcher. Quickly and carefully, they slid Jesse into it.

"Did we take the Ridge?" Jesse begged to know.

"You bet we did, Illinois," the first man answered, grinning. "The rebs are still running!" Jesse learned from them that the Army of the Cumberland had driven the rebel force off Missionary Ridge and won a tremendous victory.

They put him into a four-wheeled Medical Department ambulance. There were places in it for four wounded men, but there was only one other. His head was bloody, and he was deeply asleep and snoring loudly.

One or two hospital tents had been set up by the two doctors of each regiment about three hundred yards behind the trenches at the bottom of Missionary Ridge where they had expected most of the fighting to be. The hospital stewards brought Jesse and the other wounded man to the long row of tents where they carefully lifted Jesse out of the ambulance and laid him on a large sturdy table that stood outside one of the tents. One of the stewards cut his pants leg away, exposing his wounded leg. An officer emerged from the tent carrying a lantern, and Jesse recognized him as one of the 19th Regiment's two surgeons. He strode to the table, set the lantern down, and bent over Jesse's leg.

After poking and prodding a bit, he told Jesse, "Son, you've got a minié ball in your leg, and we need to get it out. It's not a major operation, not even any cutting required."

He gave Jesse a shot of something he called morphine, which made Jesse fall asleep quickly. He was awakened once or twice by his own heavy snoring, but only for moments, and felt no pain. He awakened completely some time in the early morning, inside the tent. His leg was throbbing, but he was glad to see it was still there. It was covered with some type of dressing that had a wet feeling to it. Jesse tried to wiggle the leg, but the sharp stab of pain he felt made him stop.

The tent held twenty beds and all but one was filled. The 19th Regiment had obviously taken at least nineteen wounded casualties, and Jesse wondered how many dead there were. The usual result of a battle, he knew, was one man dead for every four wounded, so the regiment must have had four or five men killed.

He gazed around to see if there was anyone he knew in any of the beds. Briefly, he had the futile thought that he would find Harlow. He did not see anyone he knew, but most of the men were still asleep. However, about an hour later he suddenly heard a very familiar voice call out, "Jesse! Jesse! That you?"

It was Cyrus Bolton.

Jesse raised himself on his elbows and peered about. Sure enough, some twenty feet away he saw the homely, grinning face of his pup-tent mate Cyrus Bolton looking at him.

"They got you, too, eh, Jesse? I see they got you in the leg. Looks like it's all still there, though. Glad to see that. They had to take my foot off."

Indeed, Jesse could see that Cyrus's left foot was missing. "I'm surely glad to see you're alive, though, Cy," he said.

"Aw, Jesse, I'm too ornery to get killed. You know that!" Cy said, his grin widening. But, Jesse could tell he was still in pain.

The doctor came by to see Jesse about mid-morning. "You were lucky, son," he told Jesse. "The minié ball didn't hit a bone, so it didn't flatten out. It makes a bad wound when that happens. Your ball came to a stop inside your leg and I was able to get it out with a probe." He paused a moment. "The only thing is, it left a long trail of damage through your leg. I don't know how much damage was done to some of your nerves and tendons, but it may have been serious. You may find you're going to have some trouble walking. We're going to send you to a general hospital where they'll keep an eye on you for a while."

The next day he was put into a wagon with other wounded men and taken into Chattanooga. Jesse was given a bed at a makeshift hospital and began a daily life of waiting to see what was going to happen to him. He knew that a lot of things could go wrong. Some wounded men began to run fevers and gradually wasted away until they died. Some men came down with the infectious condition called gangrene that could be fatal.

However, Jesse's wound was healing with no signs of infection. But he realized that he was going to walk with a severe limp for the rest of his life.

One day, a doctor came to see him. "Well, son," he told Jesse, "you are obviously no longer fit for military duty. I don't think you could keep up for ten minutes on a day's march. We're going to recommend you for discharge due to disability." He glanced down at a sheet of paper he was holding in his hand. "Your war is over, Jesse Bowman."

epilogue

The War Never Leaves

A few days later, Jesse was given his discharge papers and provided with a cane. They put him on a train that chugged from Chattanooga to Nashville, a short trip, then switched him to a train going to Cairo, Illinois. In Cairo they changed him to a train headed straight for Chicago. For several hours, he watched one harvested brown cornfield after another slide past in the Illinois countryside.

When Jesse got off the train at the station in Chicago, he saw that his mother and father were waiting there for him. He guessed the War Department had sent them a letter, telling them when he would arrive. His mother was actually both laughing and crying as she rushed to hug him. His father was grinning and pumped Jesse's hand. Oh, it was so good to be home! It was so good to be alive! It was now early December 1863, and he would be home for Christmas. He remembered that on his last Christmas, he had wondered if he would still be alive for this one.

For the first few days at home, Jesse found he really did not want to do much of anything. He spent a great deal of time just talking with his mother, who was very interested in the war and asked many questions about it. However, he was surprised to find that some of her questions made him uncomfortable. She asked about things he found he did not want to talk about, like what it was like to be in battle.

He quickly saw that he had not really left the war behind. Memories of things he had experienced were constantly creeping into his mind. He had nightmares of being in a battle. All the sights, sounds, and smells came back to him, mixed together in a strange senseless jumble.

Sometimes, the dreams made him sit and think about the war for hours during the day. He wondered if he would ever be able to forget it. He smiled wryly as he remembered how he had imagined war back when he was barely seventeen and fretting to enlist. He had pictured it as a child might—lines of cheering men running at each other behind flags, with bands playing music to urge them on. He had no thought of men being killed in such horrible ways. He could not have imagined, then, some of the things he had actually seen, such as a man with his body blown open and his intestines strewn about on the ground around him. He did not think he would ever be able to push such memories out of his mind.

He often wondered if anyone would ever learn what had become of Harlow Basset.

While there were many things about the war that Jesse wanted to forget, he was very much interested in keeping track of the course of the war. After all, there were still men that he knew fighting out there, and he wanted to know how they were doing. He studied every page of the newspaper every day, hoping to find some mention of the Army of the Cumberland or the 19th Illinois Infantry Regiment. He was interested in reading about the generals he had seen and served under—Grant and Thomas. They were now directing the course of the war.

Jesse finally decided he should get out of the house and move about on the city streets. He dreaded it, because he hated the thought of having people—especially young women—see him, an eighteen year old, hobbling about with a cane. However, the more often he moved among crowds, the more he became aware that there were a lot of young men on the streets who were lacking a foot, a leg, or an arm or a hand, or who, like him, were limping along with a cane. While it had long been quite common to see elderly men walking with canes, it was now quite common to see many young men walking with canes, too, as well as with crutches. He came to realize that the war had created a vast number of young men with injured bodies and that he was simply one of them.

He regretted that he would always walk with a limp, using a cane, but he was proud that he had served in the war. He firmly believed he had helped his country, but he came to accept that he would probably never forget some of the things he had seen and done during his time as a soldier, even though he might wish he could.

the end

The Real History Behind the Story

While Jesse Bowman was not a real person, the battles that he took part in really occurred during the American Civil War, which the Union won. Soldiers in the Union Army experienced many of the same things that Jesse did and helped win the war that preserved the United States of America.

The Breakup of America

On December 20, 1860, the Southern state of South Carolina announced it was no longer one of the United States; it was leaving the Union. The reason it left was that it was strongly against the election of President Abraham Lincoln, whom it thought would threaten the institution of slavery.

Suddenly, the country seemed to be coming apart. On January 9, 1861, the state of Mississippi announced it, too, was leaving the Union. Like an avalanche, the states of Florida, Alabama, Georgia, and Louisiana followed.

By February 8, the six Southern states that had announced they were withdrawing from the United States of America—"seceding" was the word they

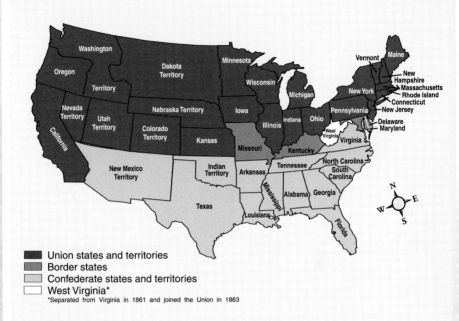

**A map of the United States at the time of the Civil War
shows the Union and Confederate states and territories.
The border states, many of which still had slavery,
remained part of the Union. West Virginia broke away
from Confederate Virginia in 1861 to become its own
state in the Union.**

used—had formed a new independent nation. They
called it the Confederate States of America, or the
Confederacy, which is actually another word for
"union." In March and April, five more Southern states
announced they were joining the Confederacy. Thus, by
the middle of 1861, the Confederacy consisted of
eleven states. Nineteen Northern states and four border

states—those located between states of the North and the South—had stayed part of the United States of America, the Union.

The Soldiers Called Zouaves

The first of the military units known as Zouaves were formed by the army of France in Morocco in the 1830s from members of a Moroccan tribe known as the Zouaoua. Their own everyday clothing of baggy red pants, a short blue jacket, and a tall red cap called a fez was adopted as their uniform. In the 1830s and 1840s, four Zouave regiments made up entirely of Frenchmen were made part of the French Army. During the Crimean War of 1854–1856—fought in Russia by France, Great Britain, and Turkey—the Zouaves won high acclaim for their courage and daring. They became very popular throughout America.

The Chicago Zouaves were organized from an Illinois State militia company by a Chicago lawyer named Elmer Ellsworth. He named them the United States Zouave cadets and trained them to perform military drills in the French Zouave manner. In July and August 1860, Ellsworth took the Zouaves on a six-week tour around the country, challenging drill teams in many cities to competitions. The Chicago Zouaves won every contest and returned home to wild acclaim.

A fellow Union soldier offers a canteen to a wounded Zouave.

On June 17, 1861, the Chicago Zouaves became the first two companies of a Union regiment that would officially be known as the 19th Illinois Volunteer Infantry Regiment, and unofficially as the Chicago Zouaves. This was the regiment that the character Jesse Bowman was in. During the Civil War, more than fifty Zouave regiments were raised throughout America, mostly in the North. The Chicago Zouaves became known as the best-trained regiment in the Union Army of the Cumberland.

The Punishment of Athens

The punishment of the town of Athens that upset Jesse so much was a real event in history. Colonel Turchin, the commander of the brigade the 19th Illinois Regiment was in, had been an officer in the Russian army and had served in European countries occupied by Russian troops. If a community in an occupied country ever tried to aid its own troops against the Russians, the Russian officers allowed their troops to assault the community, looting and robbing homes and buildings and mistreating citizens at will. This was how Turchin wanted the town of Athens punished for helping rebel soldiers attack the 18th Ohio Regiment. Doing such things to an American town was against the laws of the U.S. Army, and Turchin was court-martialed and dismissed for what he did. However, President Abraham Lincoln annulled the court-martial and Turchin returned to duty, promoted by Lincoln to brigadier general.

Military Drill

During Civil War times, drilling was the training of soldiers to make movements that were necessary for moving across a countryside or on a battlefield. Such movements included marching, changing direction while marching or standing, making the movements

This poster shows the various military drills performed by the Chicago Zouaves.

necessary to load and fire a weapon, making the movements necessary to attack or defend with a bayonet, and making the movements required for ceremonial duties. All such movements were made at the shouted command of a superior officer. For example, the command "about-face" required a man to turn his entire body completely around. The practice of learning the commands and making the movements was known as drilling.

Long Marches

Marches over long distances were carefully planned out well in advance by experienced officers. Generally, the roads picked out for use were what were called turnpike roads. They were fairly straight and were usually surfaced with gravel, which made them easier to march on than dirt roads, which often became thickly muddy in rainy weather and terribly dusty in hot, dry weather. Most turnpike roads also generally had bridges over streams and rivers.

Places where armies would camp for midday and night were always carefully selected. There always had to be a stream, river, or pond nearby where the men could get water for drinking and cooking, and it was essential to have a wooded area near where they could get twigs and branches for firewood. Such wooded and water areas were generally shown on the maps the officers used to plan the marches.

Flags of the Union Regiments

Union Army regiments carried both a national flag, called the stars and stripes, and a state flag. The national flag looked just like the national flag of today, except that it had thirty-three stars before the beginning of the Civil War, thirty-four stars until 1863, and thirty-five stars until the war's end. These stars represented

HARPER'S WEEKLY.

JOURNAL OF CIVILIZATION.

VOL. VI.—No. 299.]   NEW YORK, SATURDAY, SEPTEMBER 20, 1862.   [SINGLE COPIES SIX CENTS.
$2 50 PER YEAR IN ADVAN.E.

Entered according to Act of Congress, in the Year 1862, by Harper & Brothers, in the Clerk's Office of the District Court for the Southern District of New York.

A GALLANT COLOR-BEARER.—[See Next Page.]

The cover of the September 20, 1862 *Harper's Weekly*
showed the color bearer of the 10th New York Regiment
clinging to the American flag after receiving three wounds.

the states of both the North and South at that time. The flag had gold fringe on the edges and two gold woven tassels hanging from the top of the pole about halfway down the width of the flag.

Most state flags had a dark-blue field, but some had other colors. In the center of the field was usually an embroidery of the state seal, or coat of arms. Running across the top of the field was a gold-edged red scroll, carrying the regimental number and name in gold. The state flag also had gold fringe and tassels.

Both the national and state flags were known as the colors, and the men who carried them were generally known as the color-bearers. They held the rank of sergeant. They were especially tall and sturdy men, because the flags were heavy and unwieldy, and had to be carried steadily upright, often in heavy wind. The flags were carried in canvas cases most of the time and were only taken out when a battle was about to begin.

The men who carried the colors were highly respected by all the other men of the regiment. It was obvious that they were exceptionally brave, because they were picked out by enemy troops as the main targets to be shot at. A color-bearer was deliberately challenging the enemy to "try and get me!"

The Rebel Yell

The "Rebel Yell" was the Confederate Army's war cry. No one today knows what it actually sounded like, but many Union soldiers who heard it described it as a long, high-pitched shriek. It was used to try to strike terror into the men who were being charged by the rebel soldiers. It may also have helped give confidence to the men making the charge.

The Union soldiers also had a war cry. It was the word "Hurrah," shouted out as "Hoo-RAW, Hoo-RAW, Hoo-RAW!" as the Union soldiers rushed at an enemy position.

Battle Orders

During the course of a battle it was frequently necessary for an order to be sent from the commanding general to the commander of a regiment, brigade, or division. The order might be to move the regiment, brigade, or division to a different part of the battlefield, to go to another unit's assistance, or to make ready for an attack that was about to be made on it. The commanding general was usually in a place where he could see what was happening on most parts of the battlefield.

The general could not take the order himself, so he sent it by messenger. It was written out on a page from

158

a notebook the general usually had with him at all times. The page was given to an officer who had a fast horse and was a good rider, and he was told where to take it.

Of course, things could go wrong. The horse might get shot or stumble and break a leg, and the messenger would have to keep going on foot. This might take too long a time, and the order would arrive too late. If the messenger got shot and killed or badly wounded, the order would never get to where it was supposed to go at all. Battles were won and lost because of orders that came too late, or never came.

The Battle of Antietam in Maryland on September 17, 1862, became a defeat for the Confederate Army because of an order that was lost. The order was sent by the the commanding general, Robert E. Lee, telling the lower commanders what to do. One of them lost his copy of the order. It was found before the battle began by some Union soldiers. They took it to the commander of the Union army, Major General George McClellan, and he realized he now knew everything the Confederates were going to try to do. The battle became a Union victory that changed the course of the war, all because of a lost piece of paper!

Further Reading

Fiction

Crane, Stephen. *The Red Badge of Courage*. New York : Atheneum Books for Young Readers, 2002.

Kilgore, James. *The Passage*. Atlanta: Peachtree, 2006.

Noble, Trinka Hakes. *The Last Brother: A Civil War Tale*. Chelsea, Mich.: Sleeping Bear Press, 2006.

Steele, William O. *The Perilous Road*. Orlando: Harcourt, 2004.

Nonfiction

Anderson, Dale. *The Civil War in the West: 1861–July 1863*. Milwaukee: World Almanac Library, 2004.

Armstrong, Jennifer. *Photo by Brady: A Picture of the Civil War*. New York: Atheneum Books For Young Readers, 2005.

Bolotin, Norman. *Civil War A To Z: A Young Readers' Guide to Over 100 People, Places, and Points of Importance*. New York: Dutton Children's Books, 2002.

Rappaport, Doreen and Joan Verniero. *United No More!: Stories of the Civil War*. New York: HarperCollinsPublishers, 2006.

Internet Addresses

American Memory: Selected Civil War Photographs
<http://memory.loc.gov/ammem/cwphtml/cwphome.html>

PBS: The Civil War
<http://www.pbs.org/civilwar/>